LIZZY GAYLE

THE Blissful End

3

CITY OWL
PRESS

THE BLISSFUL END
The Djinn, Book 3

CITY OWL PRESS
www.cityowlpress.com

Cover Design by MiblArt. All stock photos licensed appropriately.

Edited by Tee Tate.

For information on subsidiary rights, please contact the publisher at info@cityowlpress.com.

Print Edition ISBN: 978-1-64898-174-6

Digital Edition ISBN: 978-1-64898-175-3

Printed in the United States of America

PRAISE FOR LIZZY GAYLE

"Gayle transports readers to an underwater utopia in *Love at 20,000 Leagues*... Devoted paranormal and sci-fi romance fans will enjoy the futuristic setting." – *Publisher's Weekly*

"A promising paranormal romance debut with intricate backstory, a fun cast of characters, and a trio of Djinn who'll have you rooting for their freedom to pursue true happily ever afters. *The Binding Stone* is a magical gem that will have readers wishing for the next in the series." – *Luna Joya, author of the Legacy series*

"I thoroughly enjoyed *The Binding Stone*, by Lizzy Gayle. What a fun, fast-paced, page-turner of a book! Leela and Jered are compelling main characters, and the supporting cast of friends, allies, and enemies keeps the story fresh and interesting. The flashbacks to Leela's long and difficult past perfectly compliment the main storyline. I can't wait for Book 2!" – *Lisa Edmonds, author of the Alice Worth series*

"Action-packed, steamy, and compulsively readable, *The Binding Stone* is a superb debut. The magic system of the story hooked me instantly... Add in romance, action, and unforgettable characters, and the author transports us to a place that is sure to enthrall any lover of fantasy." – *Kat Turner, author of the Coven Daughter series*

"Filled with magic and mayhem, *The Binding Stone* delivers a tale of twisted desires, lust for power, and a love strong enough to break the chains of betrayal." – *InD'tale*

"*Love at 20,000 Leagues* is a fast-paced, futuristic whodunit the takes place in an underwater resort called Paradise Atlantis. The story follows a woman named Sam as she faces claustrophobia, a strange pressure-related illness, and morally-ambiguous AI all while navigating a steamy love triangle...Gayle's writing is excellent and the balance between action, adventure, intrigue, and romance is spot on. This is a super fun, highly imaginative, and thoroughly satisfying read that will have you guessing right until the end. I can't wait to read the next book in the series!" – *Jess K. Hardy, author of the Ignisar series*

"The storytelling and flow of *The Bleeding Heart* is fantastic, like 'I stayed up until 5:30 in the morning finishing it because I couldn't stop turning pages' fantastic. The worldbuilding is well-paced and organic and the action picks up and never lets you down. There's action, there's twists, there's romance, and there's love – real, true, love – both familial and romantic." – *Book and Coffee Addict*

To Debbie for all your support and love.

PROLOGUE

LEELA

THIS IS THE MOMENT I'VE SPENT A YEAR LONGING FOR. PERHAPS IT IS MY nerves making me so dizzy and unsettled. For one who doesn't need sleep, I have been getting my share lately. Jered knows something isn't right, but I haven't let on the full extent of my mystery illness. I do not wish to detract from the big moment or give him or anyone else a reason to postpone for another decade.

Waves of emotion crash over me as I join hands with every Djinn I've come to know over the last millennium. Some far longer than others. Tears flow freely down my face. I could not control it if I tried. Jered, though only a magician, is able to join us as well, because of the sheer number of Djinn present, and I am forever thankful for that as he lends me his strength, enfolding me in his baby-blue aura.

Together we rise in the air, a great circle of beings with glowing eyes in the center of a cyclone of power. We fly upward, slowing time as we go so that it takes a mere flash to reach our destination. Jered has never been in space before. He will be safe with me. With us.

"It feels as though we should have a ceremony or something." Taj speaks through the connection and our minds. He is still new at leading the Order and sounds abashed, which is so unlike him. To me, that lends an air of awe to what we are doing.

"Cal will check the other side one last time," Dira says through the same connection. Her desperation to finish the work her lover started brings a pain to my heart.

Taj nods, squeezing his partner's hand, and Cal disappears through the veil. I hold my breath, but he returns mere moments later with a smile on his face.

"They are ready," Cal reports.

"Let us go through the circle one last time," Taj says, shoulders back. "Say your name and aye if you agree we should close the door permanently."

One by one, starting with Dira, our names are spoken. Every Djinn here is voting yes. It is a mere technicality. I've worked so hard for so long to convince the last stragglers of the importance of it. All I know is that I will finally be free to live a human life with the man I love. My turn can't come fast enough.

"Hold!" Mira appears in the center of our circle. She is holding the hands of Jered's stepsister Sophie and another magician I do not recognize.

Chatter breaks out, but I squeeze Jered's hand, unwilling to let go. Why has she come? Fear grips my heart and causes my palm to sweat. She said she'd stay neutral. She said she'd stay out of it.

"What's with the dramatic entrance?" Taj asks, leaning forward but not breaking the link. Though his words jest, his tone is filled with concern. Both Mira and Sophie mean so much to him. To all of us. But I will not forgive Mira if this is an attempt to stop us. I cannot let that happen. I cannot lose my one chance at happiness.

"You have to listen to me," Mira says in a booming voice that circulates throughout the circle. "You cannot close the veil."

The chatter grows too loud. I grind my teeth together in anger, still holding tight to Jered.

"You have no right!" I scream, and everyone falls silent.

Mira turns to face me, fear in her eyes and something else. Something like emerald fire. When she speaks, it is low and even, a stark contrast to my seething, trembling state. I've been tortured and abused for too long, living in the shadow of fear. I will stop that from happening ever again if it is the last thing I do.

"You did not heed my words once before, and it cost too much. You will hear me this time, Leela. I told you there were too many unknowns."

I know she speaks of her first love, Rhada, but that was centuries ago.

"If this is a way to get even—"

"No. This is to save the one I love and the ones you love, Leela. If you close that veil, then Sophie dies."

1

FIFTH WHEEL

MIRA

THE VELVET BLACKNESS OF NIGHT HIDES ME FROM VIEW AS I CREEP around the statue of Venus standing guard outside the grand entrance of the Hawaiian mansion. Clever. It's off the grid, but right smack dab in the center of Kahoʻolawe, the supposedly uninhabited island. The perfect place to keep a hidden Djinni and have them create an oasis.

I reach out with my magic and find the magician easily. They're behind the massive house in what feels like a swimming pool. But my real target is on the top level in a large space I assume is the master bedroom.

Despite my cat burglar–like appearance, I go fully invisible and transport inside.

My eyes glow as my blood boils with anger. Bile rises in the back of my throat. There are several women in the room, each one nude and bound by rope at the wrists and ankles. Three are clearly human, and their bodies display recent burns and bruises. Two are not conscious. One shakes, sobbing into the plush carpet with silent tremors. The Djinni, a petite female, smaller than my sister Leela, is bound to the bed by her wrists. Her body twists to the side, as though desperate to

hide beneath the covers, and I have no doubt that it is only our apti-
tude for rapid healing that prevents me from finding any scars on her
skin.

I turn her chains to lead and free the other women with a wave of
my hand, transporting them to a hospital in Honolulu. Then I appear
before the Djinni.

"I am here to free you. I apologize for the lead, but I have to make
sure you cannot interfere when I kill your master." I could have said
incapacitate, but let's be frank here—he's a dead man swimming.

She nods, tears filling her eyes, and lets out a small whimper. It
stings my heart. She will need much attention and care.

"How long?" I ask, voice breaking.

"Twelve years here."

"How many women?"

She looks away. "Twenty-three."

He will suffer twenty-three times over, I decide as I blink out to
finish this reign of terror.

The man is tall and lanky, his aura a disgusting mix of putrid yellow
and blood red. He relaxes in the jacuzzi, head back against a pillow
along the edge. The entire thing is surrounded by candles.

I appear behind him, and the flames of each candle burst high as
though they've become tiny blowtorches. I reach down for his hand,
resting idly on the deck and rip the large jasper ring from his body
along with his finger.

He screams, clutching his hand and twisting to face the threat as I
hold my palm open, allowing fire to consume the whole thing. A snap
frees the Djinni upstairs so I can concentrate on him.

"What the fuck—"

"No more fucking for you," I state and lift him into the air with
magic, turning him to face me. He struggles to move but cannot, and
his eyes fill with terror as I reach for his erection.

"Let me, please," a high voice says from behind me.

I turn to find the Djinni from upstairs. She is clothed in a shift dress
and holds a dagger in her hand.

I nod, backing away. "When you finish, I have placed an address in his phone." I nod toward the man who cannot even beg for his life. "Qadira will help you get back on your feet."

"I cannot thank you enough."

No doubt exists that this tiny, delicate creature is anything but a fierce survivor. I smile and disappear. I'm supposed to meet some friends.

I clean off the blood on my way to Taj and Cal's apartment. Leela and Jered are there as well when I show up.

"How'd it go?" Leela asks, bouncing over to meet me and pulling me into an awkward embrace.

"Why are there so many sadistic magicians? Is it our blood that makes them sick?" I ask, still disgusted by the assignment I just left.

"Absolute power corrupts absolutely," Taj says, handing me a stiff drink, which I gratefully down and then toss the glass back to him.

"We aren't all perverts," Jered says, pulling Leela into his arms as though being away from her for thirty seconds was just too much.

I know they aren't all bad. I've seen the extremes and everything in between.

"That's not what she said." I nod toward Leela and enjoy both their embarrassment and Taj and Cal's laughter. "So what's the plan? Something tells me that the four of you aren't sitting around playing board games on Friday night."

"We're going clubbing. Tame, I know," Cal says, giving Taj a peck on the cheek. "But dancing seems to be the one thing we can all agree on."

"Well, I won't keep you then. I promised Taj I'd pop by after each collection assignment so he knows I'm okay." I head for the door, but I'm stopped by Leela grasping my hand.

"Please join us tonight, Mir." Her entire demeanor is filled with light and joy. Jered is good for her.

I envy her carefree attitude. She deserves this, though. It is time she had a happily ever after. Taj too. A glance over at him and Caldor, hand in hand, whispering to each other, warms my heart. They've found their loves.

Mine has been dead a thousand years.

"I have work to do," I protest, trying to slip from Leela's grip.

"On Friday night? You can take a break, Mir. You need one. Come on. We're going dancing."

Jered embraces her from behind, and she leans into him. It's so natural, the look on her face pure bliss. It's physically painful to watch, but I'm not sure I'm getting out of it again. I've successfully avoided this for the past month, and I knew my time was running out.

"Fine." I sigh so she'll let go. "But just for a bit."

Leela squeals and claps her hands together in glee. "Let's find you something sexy to wear."

She practically glows, and my chest squeezes so hard I fight not to double over. Instead I force a smile in return and think longingly of the file on my desk at home beside my computer. Dira gave it to me this morning, and the excitement lighting up her eyes had been contagious.

We'd finally gotten a break on the whispers of some of the dark items available on the magician's black market. The market's existence was something the Order hadn't even been aware of until Kitra had us gather all the magicians at her island fortress with the intention of ruling them all. Turns out Cal's previous master had been involved, having procured his stone that way.

I allow Leela to drag me into Taj's master bedroom and snap her fingers, wrapping me into different outfits as I continue to think. The look on her face is touching, though, the way she sizes up whether the clothing does me justice or not before switching to the next outfit. I know she's been secretly pairing up Dira and me since we've both lost our loved ones. Sophie had been at the apartment the other day and mentioned it. It would be a tidy match, no more loose ends and single friends for Leela. But as much as I love Dira as a person, she's more like Lee and Taj—a sibling. The truth is, I can hook up with just about anyone I want, but *wanting* them is the key issue. The roller coaster of emotions and other minutia that go hand in hand with that make me exhausted just thinking about it.

I realize not finding a partner to share my new life with is a problem I've avoided, but when I think back about the two people I've allowed into my life in that way, the heartache at the end is what dwells in my heart instead of the joy of the moments we stole.

That's not how it should be. I know this. But it is a fact, and I do not care to add to this heavy burden because I may not survive another such tragedy.

Leela snaps me into a tight black minidress and heels and at last nods in approval. It's dark and not shiny, which I appreciate. My heart warms knowing she picked it for me and not herself. One look at her nearly neon pink leather and that much is clear.

"Jewelry," she mutters to herself and snaps again.

"How long is this going to take?" I ask, genuinely curious.

She shrugs. "I don't know. I still have to do your hair and makeup."

I nod, resigning myself to the makeover, and the file from my desk appears in my hand. May as well do something while I wait.

Leela makes a small noise of disapproval but continues as though nothing has happened. She won't let me get away with it while out, but she knows me. She knows that throwing myself into the work of the Order has given me a new purpose—a purpose I can handle. One where I'm helping others of our kind while not investing in anymore potential calamities of the heart.

I flip through the file, and something catches my eye. I feel the green sparks pop, making me blink, and am glad that Leela is currently behind me and unable to see the reaction. She may figure out I now have a higher purpose in joining them on the dance floor.

The mysterious mention of DB, or Djinn blood as we've come to suspect, has pinged on one of Dira's searches. Apparently, someone on a 4chan board mentioned a vial of something glowing red being passed to someone at a club in downtown LA called Aladdin. He brought it up in this space in which he foolishly felt secure, commenting that he wanted to try whatever it was. The real black-market boards were harder to access than 4chan, but those were born of actual magic and constantly slid around the Internet through time, space, and dimension. One day we'd be lucky enough to find a magician that would spill the passwords necessary to break it open.

Perhaps today would be the day.

"You know," I say, tossing the folder back through space to my desk across town, "since I'm actually going tonight, how about I pick the club?"

Leela pops in front of me, taking me in from head to toe. "As long as it's an actual club. You know, where we can all have fun."

"Ha-ha. Yes. I heard about this one in LA called Aladdin. My understanding is it's a magician club. I thought maybe it would be fun for Jered and more interesting than a regular one."

Leela narrows her vivid green eyes at me, jutting out a hip. "And this wouldn't have anything to do with a lead?"

I roll my eyes, trying not to react. "Look, if you'd rather I work..."

"Fine. We can try LA. I've never been. But you have to go like this."

A mirror materializes in front of me, and I take in her offer. Yes, the dress is black, but the earrings are about a mile long with crystals that will no doubt catch the lights of the club and make me a showstopper. I don't love attention, but it may work to my advantage tonight. My hair is sleek and loose, spilling over my shoulders and down my back to my waist at its full length because it's been straightened. My face might rival a clown, however, and herein lies the problem.

"One change," I say, snapping to remove the excess and the pink lipstick.

Leela grumbles and snaps again. My new lip color is dark red, like blood, and I look so alluring I almost want to sleep with me.

"Fine," I say, holding out my hand to shake hers. "It's a deal."

2

NIGHT ON THE TOWN

MY PLAN IS TO LET THE LOVEBIRDS GO OFF TO THE DANCE FLOOR ONCE WE materialize at the trendy club so I can stay by the bar and people-watch for any unorthodox magical activity. I enjoy taking in the show that humanity puts on after being forced to be the entertainer for so many centuries.

Taj squeezes my hand in his before we leave his apartment. I grin back, enjoying the sparkle in his emerald eyes. Love looks good on him. I wonder if heartache has soured my visage over the years.

"Ready?" he asks with a wink.

"I suppose." My sarcastic reply is more habit than accurate. But it's good if they think I'm still a grudging participant.

"I'm glad you decided to join us, Mira." This is Jered's five hundredth peace offering to me since our meeting two years ago when I tried to blow him to smithereens. It isn't that I harbor any ill will toward Leela's boy toy, but it is a bit awkward.

I nod and take his hand so we can transport directly inside the club and bypass any annoying bouncers or line at the entrance, but Taj clears his throat.

"You have a speech for us, love?" Cal teases.

"I may have taken a peek at the club Mira so uncharacteristically suggested." He glares in my direction. So much for fooling anyone, though I suppose he and Lee have known me the longest. "We'll need to enter through the front. They have magic sensors all around the building, and before you say it, Mir, yes, we can bypass as three Djinn, but why start issues with that kind of entrance in a magician's den? This is peaceful and for fun, right?"

"Of course." I hear his message loud and clear. We are not there to make trouble. No torturing magicians either. At least if he thinks that's my intent, he's off base. Unless, of course, I find one tied to the black market or, better yet, DB. Then all bets are off.

Leela tugs both physically and magically, and we fly through space as time slows. We materialize in an alleyway off a brightly lit street and break off into pairs, which in my case means me and my shadow, and stroll around the corner with Leela in the lead.

The front of the building isn't much nicer than the alley, though the neon sign that flashes Aladdin announces we're in the right spot. The building itself is two stories, concrete, and rectangular, boring as hell with no windows other than a slider on the metal door. I see the magic wards immediately, taking in the aura of yellow around the perimeter that likely makes it all but invisible to humans.

Outside, a tall magician leans casually against the wall, muscular arms folded across his broad chest. He's wearing sunglasses, which makes me chuckle to myself as we approach. I've already sized him up as one of those guys whose head is way too big for his beefcake bod. Maybe it's his copper-and-green aura, maybe it's his luscious shoulder-length black hair, or maybe it's the small smile and eyebrow raise he shoots at me when he spies me in the back of the line, acknowledging he sees something he likes.

Bet you'd like to be my master, asshole. Men like him, and women for that matter, irk me. I itch to wipe the smirk off his beautiful face. *Easy, Mir. The goal is just to get in the building.*

The bouncer barely nods as the others pass by. He may be wearing sunglasses, but I can feel his gaze on me the entire time. When he throws out a hand to stop my entrance, I make a snap decision. See if he has any information in that head of his other than how great he is.

"What? I don't pass the test?" I ask in a flirty voice, running a finger over the taut arm blocking my path.

"Maybe. Maybe not. I'll need to ask you a few questions." His voice is low and softer than expected.

"Won't that hold up the line?" I ask innocently.

"What line?"

I peer behind me, sure there had been several others that fell in behind us as we approached. Apparently, I am wrong.

"They're inside already. Regulars."

I turn back to him with my own brows raised this time. So he can transport several people? That's new for a magician. *Intriguing.*

"What's your name?" he asks, standing up straight. Thankfully, I picked a tall body when I came to Earth. Leela would probably come up to this man's nipples.

"Mira. Yours?"

"I'm asking the questions here, Mira."

"Yet it appears I am as well." I smile. I like this game. I know I can win after all.

He tilts his head. "Rook."

"Like the bird?"

"Maybe. I'll tell you more if you tell me more."

"My friends are waiting for me," I say, knowing they probably have already started dancing.

"Then you should probably let me do the asking. What brings a beautiful Djinni like you to a place like this? Aren't you scared?"

I laugh. I can't help it. "Hardly. And in case you missed it while you were ogling, I'm not the only one."

"I miss very little, Mira. That's why I needed to ask you and not them."

I swallow. Did he see something in my face? Something that betrayed my intentions here as opposed to the fun seekers I came in with? My turn to pose a question.

"And what is it you think you saw in me?"

"Depth," says Rook, and there's a beat of silence.

"Why are your eyes covered?" I ask, tempted to reach for the sunglasses for some inexplicable reason.

"I don't like to attract undue attention."

Before I can say anything else, another man slips out the door and puts a hand on Rook's shoulder. Rook doesn't look back at the man covered in black ink that swirls and writhes over his body in a mesmerizing dance. The newcomer nods at me, and I see he is Djinn.

"Thanks, Rook. You can go now."

Rook nods and opens the door, gesturing for me to enter. I remain still. And confused.

"You aren't the bouncer?" I ask, after he waits patiently in silence for a full minute.

"Nice of you to notice. Tyrannus here is the bouncer. I was watching the door for him while he attended to some personal business. Have fun with your friends."

I follow him as he strides past the brightly lit bar and between some people chatting to the side of the dance floor. He pauses as he reaches the rope across a winding metal staircase that leads up to some rooms on the second floor, and I place a hand on his left biceps, ignoring the way my attention-starved body responds to the simple touch. "Why were you asking me so many questions then?"

"Maybe I wanted to know who you are. Now I think I have a pretty good idea. See you around, Mira."

The rope disappears as he walks through it, reappearing behind him as he jogs up the steps, leaving me gaping with an excellent view of his well-formed backside.

"No snooping," Taj says from over my shoulder, making me jump. "Come on, dance with us."

He tugs on my hand, guiding me over to the dance floor where the others have joined throngs of partiers, twisting and smashing their bodies together to the sensual rhythm of the music. I don't like dancing in public. It makes me think of all the times Kitra made me do it to entertain her guests, typically ending in other forms of entertainment.

"I just want a drink," I shout, pulling away as Cal starts twerking Taj's side beneath the strobing lights.

I make my way to the bar, where I clasp my shaking hands behind me. I don't want to go there now. I don't want to go there ever. She's taken enough of my eternal life.

"What can I get you?" the bartender asks.

She's a young girl, a magician with blue hair, a bright-pink aura, and a friendly smile. She's dressed in black as well, but her shorts and halter have holes in very strategic places. I wonder if they're magicked in place.

"Hang on. I know what to get you." She winks and busies herself with a concoction that involves liquors and mixes I've never seen or heard of before, finally presenting me with a glowing blue glass. "It's a Good Intentions. It's got a spell in it. I like to state that up front."

I eye it warily. "Why is it called a Good Intentions?"

She shrugs, already mixing something for someone else. "Because you look like you got dragged here by someone with 'good intentions' and aren't having fun."

I snort, relaxing a bit. "What's the spell do?"

"Just relaxes you a little. It's nice. Try it. Some of the other Djinn like it. It's Tyrannus's fave."

I glance at the dance floor where Leela and Jered are locked together at the lips and the pelvis, moving to the rhythm. I reach for the glass and take a tentative sip. The blue liquid goes down surprisingly warm and sweet despite the ice inside.

"How do you like it? I added a little blue curaçao for flavor."

"It's nice. Thanks. What's your name?" I ask, sitting on the nearest stool and turning back to talk to the friendly girl.

"Amy." She reaches out a hand to shake before going back to serving someone at the end of the bar. Her flurry of movement makes me dizzy.

I should ask her about the DB or black market. But the question that leaves my lips isn't about either.

"What's up with Rook?"

Amy stops in her tracks for a moment, then shakes it off and keeps going. "You met him? He doesn't usually come down on the weekends. Not a big crowd guy."

"He was covering for Tyrannus," I say, taking another sip.

"Oh, right. Yeah, he's a sweet guy. He always helps out when we ask. He's the tech guy here, managing the sound system, lights, and all that. Good with magic. He's got some intricate spells I'd never even attempt on my own."

A lull in people allows Amy to finally stop her constant motion and lean across from me, wiping out some glasses and then letting them float back to the bar behind her as we talk.

I want to ask more, but I need to focus on why I came. I take another sip of my drink and lean forward. "What's your clientele like? You get any trouble around here?"

Amy laughs, a bubbly sound. "With Tyrannus out front? Hardly. Nah. Every once in a while, some cocky ass magician comes in thinking they're going to go home with one of your kind, but not in the mutual way, if you know what I mean. That doesn't last here. The regulars are like a family, both Djinn and magician. You're safe." She pats my hand, and I can't help noticing the large tourmaline ring on her hand. I stiffen.

Amy pulls her hand back, fingering it. "Oh my gosh. I'm so sorry. That's not functional. It's an heirloom. I'm not proud of it, but my grandma had a Djinni in her service. I freed him when I got the ring."

"It would be cracked if that were true." My eyes glow green with power that I find hard to control.

"Hang on," she says. "Silas!" she calls toward the dance crowd, cupping her hands over her mouth.

A man with flaming red hair pops in next to me, and when I look, I see he has the eyes of a Djinn, unnaturally bright green.

"'Sup, darlin'?" he asks Amy, not even acknowledging my presence as a threat. He isn't wearing a collar though, I notice. Or a bracelet.

"I was just explaining to this nice lady that I freed you but kept the ring." Amy winks at him and approaches a new customer to the right.

"True story," he says, holding out a hand to me and conjuring his own drink in the other. "The concern is appreciated, but Amy's a sweetheart and under my protection. I fixed the ring for her, a gift."

My eyes cool down to normal, and I shake his hand, grimacing with embarrassment. "Mira."

"Silas. Want to dance, Mira?"

I down the rest of my drink and take his hand. I can almost hear Taj's approving voice in my head and Leela's excited squeal.

3

IN THE BEGINNING

"YOU LOOK BEAUTIFUL," RHADA SAYS, STROKING THE SOFT SKIN OF MY NEW, *human arms. When her flesh touches mine, it raises tiny bumps, and a tingling sensation flows over me. A low moan escapes my lips, which makes her smile.*

"You like what I chose?"

"Very much. And I plan to explore every bit of it. But first, I want to introduce you to the world." She pulls on my wrist, tugging me forward with a smile and onto the cobbled street outside her small home.

"I'd rather you keep touching me like that," I say in all honesty, taking in the multicolored tiles and curved entryways all around us. "It's all so strange here."

"Strange and wonderful," she says, throwing her head back and inhaling the dry, warm air like it is a delicacy.

The pleasure on her face, the way her thick eyelashes dust the swell of her cheeks, the curve of her breasts beneath her dress, it all pulls me in so that I am no longer interested in the strange place surrounding us, only in following Rhada anywhere.

"Come on..." She tugs again, and her smile is contagious.

We run through the streets, laughing at the simplest things and completely carefree. I like the way my body feels beneath my clothing and the way I move with balance and grace. I could run and dance for hours.

We make it to a marketplace where carts line up along the sides of the walkways. They're filled with wares of unimaginable colors and textures. The sounds of other people, humans, chatter around us, and they call to us from their carts, vying for our attention.

"Come, lovely ladies! Try this new material from the Orient."

"These ladies are looking for jewels to complement their beauty."

"Taste these fresh pomegranates. They will stain your lips red with their sweet, juicy seeds."

"What's a pomegranate?" I ask as Rhada pulls me toward the intoxicating scent.

She holds up a rounded fruit and hands the man there some shiny bits of metal.

Rhada breaks open the fruit as we meander along the never-ending market that snakes along the streets of the small town. She hands me a half and shows me to how scoop out the seeds. When I place them in my mouth, the flavor makes me gasp with pleasure and groan as I swallow. When I open my eyes, I find her staring at me, mouth ajar.

"Such a temptation," says a deep voice from behind.

I turn to find a man cloaked in fine silks and turban. He is shorter than I am and has a long, oily braid down his chin. Rhada takes my hand, and she tugs me away.

"Did you leave the brothel?" he asks, stepping forward to meet my retreat. "Surely they are not teaching young women to behave so brazenly in the market these days."

"She is new here," Rhada says, clasping my arm so tight that an unpleasant sensation lingers. This time I frown. "I will teach her the ways, sir."

"I believe, perhaps, I should take that job on myself."

This time I call out in pain when Rhada's nails dig into my arm, drawing droplets of dark-red pain from my skin.

The man takes my other hand and pulls me harshly to his side. "Walk behind me and follow me to my home where I will teach you the appropriate places to enjoy yourself," he commands.

I look to Rhada. I do not understand what is happening.

Taj appears from seemingly nowhere at her side where he grasps her hand and smiles at the man in front of me. "I see you've met my sister Mira."

The man releases my arm, scowling at me as though Taj has just threatened him. "Indeed. Do not allow her to wander too far unchaperoned. If someone else had seen what I had, it could have been dangerous for the girl. I am considering enacting a veil law for the village, to protect the innocent from gawking men."

"Or perhaps you can enact a law that suggests such men learn to control themselves and their urges." Taj reaches his free hand for me, and I take it. I like that his hand is large and warm, but the bumps I felt with Rhada do not appear.

"Kitra!" the man calls, turning toward the market. He calls the name so loud that I startle, but Taj holds tight to my hand. "Where is that child?"

"Here, Father." A beautiful young woman appears at his side. She could be Djinn, except her eyes are a deep brown, the color of the sand when a rare storm floods the ground. Those eyes train on a spot over my shoulder, and I glance over to find Rhada staring, breasts rising and falling too rapidly.

I find myself wanting to interrupt the moment and steal back her attention. But I chide myself for being silly and so new in my human body.

"Return to the house. And from now on, you will wear a veil in public," he mutters. His daughter rolls her eyes as he moves away before following toward a hill beyond the market. But before she goes, she gives Rhada one last look, running the tip of her pink tongue over her full lips.

"Looks like someone is interested in playing a dangerous game," Taj says after the humans are out of sight.

"Dangerous is fun. Don't you agree?" Rhada asks, green eyes sparkling and dark curls bouncing against her back.

Taj grins. "The best, unless you're parading a brand-new Djinni around a crowded marketplace with a man like Sakhr in charge. Do be careful. I like this area. I'd rather not have to leave because you lose it and burn the place down."

Taj disappears, and I pull Rhada toward me, pouting. "I think I've had enough sight-seeing for one day. I'd like to go home and explore some more of what this body can do."

4

QUEEN TO ROOK 5

Silas laughs as he dances, appearing so relaxed at Aladdin that it makes me feel even more out of sorts than usual. My own paranoia stands out like a magician in a sea of humans as I fight to keep track of everyone and everything around me while I move in tandem with him. I like the body he's chosen with his ginger hair and beard. He reminds me of the pictures I've seen of the human prince, which I find amusing as he twirls and sways before me, emerald eyes crinkled in delight.

I envy Silas with his carefree attitude and wonder how long he'd been in service of a magician. Surely he wouldn't behave this way if he'd been through the torture we had. I don't begrudge him though. I am happy that some of our kind were not scarred as deeply as others.

"So what brings you out here?" he shouts over the music.

I glance over at my companions still dancing and having a wonderful time of their own. I suppose having someone to share the time with has given them the freedom to do so. "My friends thought I needed a night out."

Silas laughs again, and I can't help but smile at the loud, carefree sound that bursts from his lips. He grabs my hand and twirls me out and then back in to capture me in his embrace. It's shocking, feeling his body pressed against mine, but also not uncomfortable. Just...neutral.

You are tense. I can attest to that, he says through the connection between us. I appreciate that because his voice is both soft and clear this way.

I let out a sound that's almost a laugh. "It's hard to let your guard down when you've been through what I have."

Silas pulls me in and leans his head against mine, sliding his hands up and down my back as we sway. *Maybe I can help work out some of those knots for you.*

Ugh. This is what I get for allowing myself to try. Maybe it's not a total waste. Perhaps I can manipulate the situation to get some information.

What are those rooms upstairs for? I purr in his head.

His excitement swells between us, and I know I have him.

They're apartments. One is Amy's, and I'm sure we can use it. She's working until close.

I contemplate my options. I have no intention of actually sleeping with this Djinni, and he hasn't done anything out of line. I don't want to be cruel, but I do want to trace the magician's black market. It seems unlikely that Djinn would be involved, however. What would they stand to gain from selling their own blood and creating more magicians, more danger?

I'm not ready for that much R&R, yet. I pull away, smiling apologetically, but continue to dance.

"Let me know if you change your mind." He spins me back and forth, regaining his lighthearted demeanor of before.

"I will," I shout back.

He pulls me in again, this time, my back against his front side as we dip and sway our hips in unison.

I glance up at the thin balcony at the top of the metal stairs to find Rook leaning on the banister, and despite his dark glasses still in place, I can feel his gaze burning right through me. A flush works its way up through my body from my toes to my face, and there's no blaming it on my dancing.

He's the one I need to question. I feel it, some weird connection between us, and I need to know what it is. He's a magician, a human, and I've never seen him before in my long life; that I'm sure of, so why do I feel this pull?

He nods slightly from his perch up high, as though he's read my mind, and I nod back, a smirk crawling across my face. The promise of a challenge rises in my chest and between my legs because I find nothing sexier.

"I need another drink." I make my excuse, grab another glass of blue courage from Amy, who has it ready in under a minute, and take a sip.

Silas has been swallowed by the crowd again, and more people have joined the throngs throughout the club, making my ascent up the steps undetectable. It doesn't hurt that I turn myself literally invisible as I go, I suppose, but I don't need Uncle Taj getting in my way.

I appear again, sipping my beverage beside Rook, who now relaxes against an open doorframe at the top. He doesn't flinch, simply crooks the corner of his mouth upward in greeting.

"None for me?" His voice is low, but I hear him clearly.

I conjure a second and hand it to him as I find myself swaying to the music filling the space.

"I suppose you want to come in?" He steps aside, but remains in the entryway so that I brush against him as I pass through.

"I'll take that as an invitation," I say, but he's already shutting the door behind him.

His apartment is small but comfortable and well insulated from the sound of the club. I assume it's magical since it's so complete, but it makes sense for those that live above such chaos. The noise must become tedious. There is a living space decorated with modern leather sofas with buttons and cords running from their sides. They represent the latest technology and likely do various things like charge phones and recline. There's a small kitchen with an open breakfast bar and two stools in the corner, far too many plants for the image I'd built of him in my mind, and two doors presumably leading to a bathroom and bedroom. I catch him watching me as I glance at them.

"So," he says, sitting on the center of the sofa and crossing his legs. "Tell me what you've figured out about me, Miss Mira."

I finger the long leaf of a succulent on the counter. "I know you work here and are a tech expert."

"Boring," he says and takes a sip of his drink.

"And that you don't watch TV because there is none." I gesture to the wall that would obviously hold a flat-screen, but instead it has a painting of a rainforest.

"Or it's in the bedroom." He gestures over his shoulder at one of the doors as he uncrosses his legs, sets down his drink, and leans forward.

I shrug. "I doubt it. I also know you crave nature."

"All obvious," he says with a tsk. "I'm disappointed. Anything else?"

I grin and saunter toward him until my knees press against his. "One more thing, though I suppose that's obvious too."

He raises his eyebrows in question as I lean down, flashing my own drink to the counter so that I can slowly draw the sunglasses off his face. He does an excellent job remaining still, but the increase in breath and the rapid rise and fall of his chest give away his reaction. The eyes that look back at me draw a small gasp from my lips. I've never seen such a color on a human before, almost like small facets of glowing amber are imbedded in his irises. But the beauty is shrouded in a hazy cloud that can mean only one thing.

"You're blind." What I meant to say is *You want me.* But the shock of the discovery and his allowance of my touch replaced the words.

"How did you know?" he asks, voice soft like velvet.

I sink to my knees, straddling his lap on the sofa as my tiny dress rides up to my hips. "You use magic to see?"

He nods, his hands finding the outside of my bare thighs. His touch sets a fire low in my belly that flares to every extremity. "But not like you do. I could fix it, or have some Djinn friends do so, but it's part of who I am. I don't need it to change. I like myself."

I like him too, though I cannot explain why. Perhaps because any other man, Djinn or otherwise, would have already been groping me. His hands have stayed infuriatingly put on my thighs, driving me crazy.

"How do you know what I look like? That I am Djinn?" I ask.

"I see energy. Djinn have an emerald aura. Yours is different though."

"How so?" I ask, pressing forward so that my chest mashes against his rock-hard pectorals.

His breath washes over my face, sending the enticing scent of whisky and tobacco. "It's clear and beautiful, swirling in a mesmerizing rhythm like music. But it's held so close to your body that I can see every curve. You play it close to the vest, but you're basically naked to me."

He slides his hands slowly and delicately over my flesh and up to the edge of the material of my dress. A pulse of desire shoots between my legs, and my own breath speeds to match his.

"Then it's only fair if I get to see you naked too."

I meant to ask about the black market or the Djinn blood. But I can barely focus, and if I don't get those big hands moving over me soon, I'm going to move them myself.

"Not on the first date," he says, his fingers telling a different story as he slips them over my nearly bare ass, running dangerously close to where I straddle him.

"I never called this a date." My lips are right over his, and it's almost impossible to resist finishing the distance, this dance making me ache for him in ways I haven't experienced in many years. Is it the Good Intentions drink that I've had two of? Or is it something else? Something about Rook?

We stay like that for far too long, neither of us willing to make the first real move that will bring us to the realm of no return. He may be the most stubborn, yet strongest man I've ever encountered.

"Why did you come up here?" he asks, moving one of his hands up to take hold of the base of my neck. Perhaps to prevent me from pulling away. I wouldn't, though. I admit I am enjoying this way too much.

"You intrigue me," I say, copying his comment from earlier.

"It's more than that," he says, guiding me forward until his lips brush mine so lightly that I'm left only with longing and tingles that draw an actual moan from me. But he holds my head steady so that I don't press forward.

The message reads: *If you want more, I will give it to you in exchange for the truth.* But I'm supposed to be the one doing that to him.

"I agreed to come to find information," I say. "About a magician's black market and some dangerous things they are trading in."

My heart thumps against him, unable to hide. He could probably see it in my energy anyway. In response, he pulls me in and parts his mouth against mine. I run my tongue along the tip of his, drawing out a moan of his own. I swipe deeper, encouraging a mutual dance of exploration as we tangle together, unable to get enough. He strokes the side of my cheek with his finger and glides his other hand upward over the curves of my body to my breast where he circles his thumb over my nipple, already hard and obvious through the thin material of my dress.

I'm lost, and it's wonderful. His generous erection strains against the material of his pants, rubbing just the right spot, and I slide my hips over him, stroking with my body in ravenous need for something long buried by my conscious mind.

He groans and pulls his head away, letting it drop against the couch as I continue to work against him and run my tongue down the curve of his neck, nipping at the exposed flesh.

"Stop or I won't be able to control myself," he says, head rocking back and hips thrusting to meet me. "And neither of us wants this to be over so fast."

It takes effort to stop my body from moving and climb off him, but I do it for the promise of more enjoyable things to come. He lifts me into his strong arms and carries me to the closed door behind us, kicking it open with his foot.

I'm attached to him at the mouth as he lowers me to the bed, and I remove his clothing with a snap of my fingers. He stands, breathing raggedly and running a hand through his luscious black locks. I enjoy the beauty of his hard-earned muscles that for a Djinn would be easy, but a human not so much. His shoulders are broad and his body strong, but perfectly proportioned. His skin is smooth and a shade darker than my own, sporting a dark tattoo that wraps over his shoulder, chest, and back—a bird of prey. His erection waits proudly, anticipating more.

While he catches his breath, I glance at his bedroom, expecting more plants, but what I see is a workstation set up along the entire wall with several monitors and controls. The biggest screen shows a view of the club below, and I assume is for the lighting and such. But the one next to it gives me pause because of its vintage look right out of the 1980s.

DOS script scrawls across the tan screen of a fat little monitor, the cursor at the bottom blinking below the initials DB. I swing my head back to find Rook staring at me with his empty amber eyes, fear written clearly across his face and his erection deflating.

"You said you were looking for info on the black market. Well, you came to the right guy."

5

WHY ME?

I STAND AND TUG MY DRESS BACK INTO PLACE. NORMALLY I'D BE ECSTATIC to break this open. I'd have a million questions to demand answers to. Those questions still exist, and burn to be asked, but they all dry up on my tongue, and I stand like I'm as mute as he is blind, waiting I suppose for an explanation. Something that will tell me this isn't what it looks like.

"Can I have some clothes back?" he asks again, running a hand through his hair.

I snap, and he's wearing pants again. But I leave him shirtless. I remain quiet and still. I don't want to hurt or even threaten to hurt this man who so easily broke through my carefully constructed walls and breathed life back into the part of me I feared to open. I cross my arms.

He nods as though understanding that he must do the talking now.

"I created it about a dozen years ago, and it just took off. My magic is tied to technology, which I think is a result of my father being a computer scientist. So from a young age, I learned about both magic and technology."

There's a lump in my throat the size of the Taj Mahal, and I can't seem to form words as Rook pulls over the sliding chair and sits. He walks the rolling chair over to me and places his hands on my hips, looking up at me from below, pleading with his expression.

"I'll tell you whatever you want to know, Mira. I don't know what you think this is, but it's nothing bad. I've grown up among both Djinn and magicians, and I am against violence."

I collapse onto the edge of the bed, not trusting my legs to hold my weight any longer. He wheels toward me again, closing the distance to take my face in his hands. My eyes glow green. I feel the hot prick that means it's happening. He should be afraid, but he isn't, or at least doesn't act like it. Maybe he can't see it. Or maybe he does, and for some crazy reason, he trusts me. Well then, he's obviously too trusting for his own good. Perhaps that's how others have taken advantage of this thing he created.

I glance at him and know immediately it isn't the case. This man before me is not as naïve and trusting as Jered. His face, his attitude, the simple way he carries himself tells the story of someone who has seen too much of the world, despite his claimed happy upbringing. I've come to know the look over my centuries on Earth. It's one that is as distinct as the eyes of a Djinni.

"It is my mission, Mira, to bring knowledge of magic to the world. I want the information to leak, but I'm no fool. I know that doing so quickly will open things both too fast and potentially give the wrong people the opportunity to take control."

I want to believe him. But even if I do, it's a bad idea. There's also the matter of the blinking cursor over his shoulder. The one that highlights the initials of something very dangerous.

"Djinn blood," I whisper. The first words since learning Rook's connection to the black market. "The wrong people have already gotten a hold of it, and by the looks of it, you already know that."

Rook doesn't blanch. "Wrong. Djinn blood is the key to fixing the problem. It's taken willingly, and the more we spread both the knowledge of magic and the magic itself around, the easier it will be for everything to normalize and bring peace to the Djinn and magicians."

My heart squeezes, and I am glad he cannot see the tear escape to trickle down my cheek. I can read the hope in both his face and his aura, which doesn't lie. He believes what he says.

"Rook, you can't believe that creating more magicians is the answer. It simply creates more danger for us." I put a hand on his arm, unable to keep myself from physical contact despite the reality of what I've learned.

He smiles, and it undoes me. I want to cry because he honestly thinks he's done us a service of some sort.

"I have," he says, and I startle.

"Have what?" I ask.

"Done *us* a service." He repeats the words plucked directly from my thoughts.

Fear bristles inside me for the first time since meeting him, but I tamp it down immediately. Instead I pull my hand away and speak again with my mind.

How do you hear me?

"I don't know how it works exactly," he says in answer, despite our lack of physical contact. "And before you ask, no, I couldn't hear you at first. Not until we were connected on my sofa."

I've never met a magician with that kind of power before. As much as I want to trust this man, all the evidence is telling me otherwise.

"I'm leaving." I stand, forcing him to roll back away from me.

He watches with blank and beautiful eyes as I walk to the doorway and pause.

"I'm going to have to dismantle the network."

Rook draws in a sharp breath and stands between me and the tech behind him. "Please, Mira, don't do this. Give me a chance to show you, to explain more."

I shake my head, opening my mouth to tell him there's no point, but the words dry up on my tongue. I press my eyes closed and steady myself.

"I work for the Order of the Djinn," I say, unable to look at him. "Our purpose is to dismantle any threat to the Djinn. That includes freeing those enslaved as well as stopping things that pose a threat like what you've created, Rook. I know you don't see it, but there's too much danger in your plan."

I feel him come close, his warm, intoxicating breath washing over me as he tries to control his emotions. I keep my eyes closed. I don't want to see his broken expression. I don't want to crush his hard work. But I have to.

"What's the alternative, Mira?" he asks, and my eyes snap open. "Without risk, there's no gain." He takes my hand in his, holding it over his heart. "Your Order keeps freeing Djinn as fast as they're taken? Or we make it normal for Djinn and magicians to coexist? Humans too. Maybe it's time for a forced evolution of sorts so everyone catches up."

"We close the curtain between worlds," I say. I don't mean to let it spill out, but it's what Leela talks about incessantly. "Then we become the same and take away the danger."

Rook takes a step back, leaving me feeling cold.

"What makes you think we become the same? That sounds even more dangerous to me."

"Djinn choose which side of the veil they wish to reside on. It's a conscious decision of all of us. No one forces a choice like you'd have us do."

Rook tosses his hair back from his shoulder. "I'm not choosing for anyone. I'm spreading awareness of something that never should have been kept secret at all."

"I'm sorry. I can't allow this to continue." I wave a hand outward, intending to destroy the web he's built.

Rook catches my hand, and the force of his protective magic hits me like a wave. He's somehow managed to block my strike in such a powerful way that I would have been knocked off my feet if he hadn't grabbed me.

My eyes widen as he releases my hand.

How did you do that?

"I'll tell you over dinner tomorrow," he says, his alluring smirk returning to his face as he snaps, and his sunglasses appear once again, obscuring his secret.

"This isn't a game." I enjoyed the one we played earlier, but that was before I realized he was a magician of dangerous power and the mastermind of the elusive black market I've been chasing. How do I even know for certain that he can't consciously control his own aura?

"No, it isn't a game. That's why I can't let you destroy what I've built."

"Don't make me do something I'll regret. I can't allow this, Rook."

He cocks his head at me. "I'll tell you what, Mira the Djinni. If you give me the weekend to explain and still don't agree, I will willingly take it all offline. I'll even shut things down temporarily until we talk and blame it on a bug in the system."

I hesitate, glancing between him and the orange cursor on the screen behind him. Then his hands are on my shoulders, and his mouth covers mine again. My body reacts like there's no alternative, opening to him and his touch as though it's been craving this for centuries. Perhaps it has, and he knows it. But the electricity between us is undeniable.

I run my fingers through his silken hair and suck on his bottom lip as I pull away, breathless.

"Fine. But you give me access to it so I can monitor that you're telling the truth." I hand him my phone.

He breathes heavily again as he takes it, letting his aura wash over it in a multitude of colors before handing it back.

"I'll pick you up at seven tomorrow. Your place."

"You don't know where I live." I smile.

"Oh, I'll find you." And he buries my next question in another tidal wave of a kiss.

6

IN THE BEGINNING

RHADA'S HUMAN HANDS AND TONGUE ARE INSTRUMENTS OF PLEASURE. SHE teaches me the parts of my own body and what they are capable of with both until I am nearly unconscious from the energy I've spent. Then I have a turn practicing on her, feeling her silky skin and tasting her honeyed aroma in the liquid on my tongue as I press between her folds. Her body shakes beneath me as I hold her knees pried open to explore to my heart's content.

It amazes me that such a tiny nodule of flesh can bring so much sensation to a body. I rub at it with my thumb rapidly, applying the kind of pressure I enjoyed when she'd done so to me. And it is so much fun to feel her uncontrollable trembling when she hits her point of no return. The moans she releases make me keep pressing and rubbing to see how long I can draw the sounds out of her.

When we finish, we embrace, flesh against flesh on the bed of silk and feathers she has procured, exploring each other's mouths just as fully.

She rests her hand on my breast, tracing lazy circles around my erect nipple and reawakening the urges between my legs. How one part of me affects another so strongly is yet another mystery of the human condition.

"You are an excellent lover," she murmurs, pulling at my earlobe with her teeth.

"Oh? And how many have you been with to compare?"

Rhada's deep laugh reverberates through both of our bodies. "Several. Are you jealous?"

"I don't know. I think that's what this feeling is. You are mine, and I am yours."

"Yes. But we are Djinn. Humans are nothing, playthings that make us feel good. Toys. I expect you to play as well. Learn so we can teach each other."

"I don't want to." I pull away to sit and stretch.

"Did you enjoy what I did to you? What you so eagerly learned to do back to me?" she asks, smiling up at me like she knows a secret I do not.

Blood rushes to my cheeks as I whip around to face her. She behaves as though she knows so much more than I do. It has not been more than a human year she and Taj have been gallivanting around in these bodies. It is but a moment to us.

"Of course I enjoyed it. But I think we know enough now. And isn't it careless to play with these creatures like that?"

"Oh, my beautiful Mira, I assure you they enjoy every moment of it. I'll show you." Rhada waves, and a human appears in the room between us, swinging his head back and forth as though he doesn't know where to look.

"Kush, it's lovely to see you again." Rhada climbs onto her knees to take his shoulders in her hands. She kneads his muscles, and the tension melts out of him.

I am frozen, facing him as he drinks in my naked body, lust glazing over his eyes. His face is not alluring to me, though his body is intriguing with its sharper angles and broader build. Mira has taken his clothing as well, and my gaze is drawn downward where the angle of his waist disappears down into a tumble of black curls and the large male appendage pointing straight into the air.

I watch, swallowing as Rhada's hands stray past his shoulders and down over his chest to this very spot, gripping the length of it and stroking. Kush groans as she continues to touch him, peering over his shoulder at me, her own eyes filled with want.

"Kush, this is my friend Mira. I want you to teach her what a man can do for a woman."

My pulse speeds up, extra blood rushing everywhere and not just my head. The tingle that sparked when Rhada touched me sparks again. It's a *strange feeling, watching this moment between them, the woman I love and her human toy, for my own benefit. I feel powerful, embarrassed, and far more jealous than before. But there is also a sense of curiosity that makes me lick my lips as she releases him from her grip and shoves him toward me.*

"I don't need a man. I need you," I say, freezing him midstep.

She snaps, and he comes back to life. "This pleases me. I want to watch."

Kush pulls me toward him, mashing my body against his, his appendage poking my stomach as he kisses me roughly, squeezing my breast.

"Slow down." Rhada laughs from behind, and he lifts me and tosses me onto the bed beside her.

She looks down at me, brushing hair away from my face as he lies over me, taking my nipple between his teeth and circling it with his tongue. I gasp as his other hand finds the spot of flesh between my legs, expertly rubbing it and dipping a finger between the folds.

Rhada leans down and kisses me deeply, stroking my free breast as well, and my hips arch high on the bed. Two fingers slide inside me now, slipping with ease now that my body has decided to obey Rhada's wishes.

Kush pulls out and angles his length at my entrance, now hungry for more attention. Rhada's fingers replace his at my sensitive spot as he squeezes slowly into my core.

I grunt as he fills me and then moan as he pulls away. I don't want him to take it out.

"More," I say.

He thrusts it in again and then again, never fully pulling out, and my body moves with him, welcoming the sensation I cannot label. All I know is the spot he reaches deep inside coupled with Rhada's touch sends me quickly into uncontrollable bliss.

He empties himself and rolls off as my body shudders with release.

"Good, right?" Rhada asks, still leaning over me.

I nod, at a loss for words. "You are still more than enough."

She kisses me again, tracing the edge of my teeth with her tongue before drawing back. "I like playing with both men and women, and I'm glad you do too. Some people don't like both, Taj for example. I wanted to experiment with him too, but he rejected the idea."

I furrow my brow. I do not find the idea of Taj doing what Kush just did appealing. It feels...wrong. So I'm quite happy that he decided not to give in to Rhada's demands.

I watch as Kush climbs up behind Mira, his hands coming around the front of her, one slipping between her legs and the other rolling her nipple between fingers.

"Mmmm," she moans, shutting her eyes with pleasure. I watch as Kush enters her this time, but from behind, disappearing inside her.

I slip off the bed as she bounces on top of him, bodies writhing in a sensual dance. I do not wish to see anymore. Though I doubt I will ever get the image from my mind. I scoop up my clothing and close the door quietly behind me, fighting back the bile rising at the back of my throat.

She cannot say I refused to try what she wanted. And it felt good while it was happening. But now that he was inside her, all I feel is ill. Human emotions are confusing, and I wonder if perhaps I made a mistake in joining her here.

7

MY DATE

I EXPECTED LEELA AND TAJ TO TEXT ME, BUT WHEN I GOT ONE FROM CAL, I had to roll my eyes. They knew I left—it wasn't like I hadn't warned them—but it also wasn't as though I planned to hang around in Aladdin after leaving Rook's apartment. They also knew I'd been upstairs with someone, Taj pointing out my swollen lips and mussed hair, so I suppose they were looking for details.

It's none of their business. I learned a long time ago that my love life was my own, and I had no desire to share with anyone. So I busy myself with flipping through various files for the Order and chatting with Dira on Slack, though blowing off her questions about any leads on DB.

I glance at the clock, grimacing when I see it's only four thirty in the afternoon. I wish I could speed time up as well as slow it down. Then I reread the first page in the file on the newest Djinni we have to free. She's in a hotel in Zurich at the moment. I should assign Leela because I know she enjoys freeing our people, but I can't seem to focus on the words before me.

We're down to the last six. Dira's message pops up in the corner window on my screen.

My fingers hover above the keyboard, my heart rate speeding up. The last six Djinn. The last six that we've traced to active masters. That makes everything very real all of a sudden. I recall Taj speaking to the group when he'd officially taken up station as the leader of the Order. He'd paced back and forth in the front of Dira's living room, magically enlarged to hold us all comfortably on the couch. Then he'd faced us, tears in his eyes as he'd spoken.

"We have narrowed the list down to seventeen magicians still in possession of Djinn. We haven't had a new ping from our sensors in over a month."

Leela had jumped from the couch at this point. "That means it's almost time."

Taj nodded. "According to Faiz, the optimum time to close the door between worlds is coming in a little over a year. That gives us a timeline with which to work. We need to divide up the list and take one or two at a time, until everyone is free. If we do that, and everyone is in agreement, we can move forward with the plan."

I could see the nervousness in Taj's body language. He was as uncertain as I was about the very real issues that could be involved in closing the door. But Leela was—*is* so adamant, that our doubts are all but outweighed by her passion.

It's not like I blame her for wanting it to end so she can sleep at night in security next to the person she loves.

Six more Djinn to free. Six more for Leela to persuade. I don't doubt for a second that she will. That means I have to decide sooner than I'd like to think about where I plan to stay. I love Taj and Leela as a family should. But do I fear this world more than I love them?

I sigh, type back a thumbs-up, and shut down the computer. I'm a fool for believing I could concentrate when I keep feeling his lips on mine. He likely will not find me as he professed. The much more probable outcome is that he has tried to run and I will have to hunt him down. It will not be that difficult now that I know him and I've had access to his magical signature that he left on my phone. Even if he makes it disappear, I've felt it. I've accomplished much harder tasks at a master's beck and call. My plan is to visit his apartment over Aladdin at 7:01 p.m.

Still, I get ready as though I'm going on an actual date, which is almost laughable. But I have to fill the time somehow, so I shower and take my time picking out an outfit as though Leela is here helping me. I imagine her commentary as I try on the possibilities.

"Too prudish. Too little left to the imagination. Too off-putting. Too dominatrix." I smile at my mirror image in the black leather pantsuit and thigh-high boots. I wonder what Rook will think of this?

"I like it very much," he says from my bedroom doorway.

I swing toward his voice, ready to lash out with a burst of power, but he stands there, leaning against the doorjamb with a bouquet of purple irises in his hands.

He's more beautiful than I remember, in his gray poet's shirt and tight jeans. His hair is pulled back into a ponytail, and I imagine twisting it around my hand as we kiss.

"Not yet," he says with his quirked-up lip. "I promised to convince you not to dismantle my web first."

He stands and strides inside to meet me like he owns the place. It both angers me and turns me on. I take the flowers and toss them toward my dresser where a vase filled with water appears holding them.

"You're good at distracting me," I say, trying not to think about being unnerved by his ability to hear others' thoughts that even I cannot mimic.

"It's not everyone, only a few people over my lifetime that I've been able to hear like this. It's almost as disconcerting to me. It's always been people I'm close to. There's something about you, Mira."

"I bet you say that to all the women you almost bed." I decide to stay in the black leather outfit and lead the way out to my sitting area.

"It's not like I haven't fucked before," he says from behind me. "But no. I've never had this happen with another person."

"Well, have you fucked a Djinni?" I ask, spinning on him. I don't know where that came from or why I'd need to know his personal history.

"A person is a person, Mira." His voice is so gentle and almost sad that his response angers me.

"Maybe it has to do with our magic. Maybe it has nothing to do with you." I poke him in the chest. I know it isn't about some crazy love connection between us. I'm not that naïve.

"You're beautiful when your eyes burn green." He kisses me before I register that he's spoken as though he's seen my eyes glow. This time he speaks in my mind like another Djinn through our physical connection.

I see your magic, remember? It's breathtaking. You're breathtaking.

And then I see it in my mind's eye, his perspective of me, and it is truly beautiful. It's my essence tucked into the shape of my body as though we were beyond the curtain and viewing it with human eyes.

Our bodies mesh together like they were molded for each other, our tongues exploring every bit of each other's mouths.

I thought you wanted to prove something first, I challenge. *Perhaps distracting me is all you are capable of.*

Rook pulls away, taking a step back as his ponytail slips from my hand. He licks his lips. I drift my gaze downward; that bulge in his tight jeans can't be very comfortable.

"I don't usually lose control like this." He cocks his head, studying me.

"I guess I have that effect on people." I sit on the arm of my lounge chair. "Where are we going?"

Rook holds out his hand for me, and I take it. I can't help but appreciate the feeling of his grip, secure and warm in my own. He twists into space, slowing time, and pulls me toward Los Angeles. This time we don't stop at Aladdin. Instead, he takes me farther along to streets overflowing with homeless men and women, makeshift tents and boxes set up as homes line the sidewalk surrounded by piles of garbage and haphazard belongings. The stench of human sweat and feces makes me gag.

"Skid row?" I ask. Not the first place I'd think of for a date.

Rook pulls me forward on human legs toward a man warming himself over flames coming from a trash can. The man has a scraggly beard and a mishmash of too-big clothing layered on him, as well as a knit cap that was probably made for a woman as it's too tight on his head and bright pink in color. He has a magician's aura around him, but it's gray and dark, which makes me sad. His eyes are kind though when he looks up at us. They're filled with recognition as he settles on Rook.

"Hey, Pops, I wanted you to meet someone. This is Mira. Mira, my father."

I hold back my surprise as Pops swallows my hand in both of his own, covered in grime and fingerless gloves.

"She's a beauty, son. It's a pleasure to meet you, Mira."

"Likewise, I'm sure." I have so many questions. Why he allows his father to live in squalor is at the top.

"Pops raised me after I ran away from home at the age of ten," Rook says, handing the man a fresh hotdog that he conjured out of nowhere.

"I thought you said you were raised happily with magicians and Djinn that love each other or some such nonsense." I hand Pops a large bottle of water to wash down his dinner.

"I was. See, my birth parents fought all the time. They loved each other at the beginning, but when I showed signs of unusual magic, they started blaming each other, and believe me, when two beings of their strength fight, it's overboard."

"I'm sorry," I say, and I mean it as I can well picture two strong magicians battling using magic with an innocent child in the middle of it.

Rook shrugs. "I knew it was all about me. Neither of them cared to deny it, so I ran away. Luckily, Pops here found me before some of the more dangerous elements down here did. He and our family protected me, raised me with love. They taught me that magic didn't equate to being better than anyone else or even to money and power. It just...was."

"But surely if there are magicians down here, they wouldn't choose to live like this. They could use their magic to at least find shelter and a home."

"This is my home," Pops says, swallowing the last of his water. "I've helped a lot of people in my life. No place better to find them than where the needy end up." He winks at me.

"So you choose this in order to help others? But surely there must be easier ways to accomplish that."

"You have to go to the heart of the issue if you want something to change." Pops pats me on the arm and turns back to his trash can.

"You'd be surprised at the number of magicians that end up in places like this," Rook says in his calm way.

"But they have power."

"Greed is the most destructive force there is," Pops says from behind me.

"Ready for stop number two?" Rook draws my attention away from the odd magician in front of me. "I only have the weekend after all."

I take his hand, and he tugs again, this time pulling me back to the club as I originally expected. We land in his apartment between the bed and the tech display across from it. A warm feeling floods my chest when I see that the equipment is untouched since yesterday, the screens exactly as I left them.

"A promise is meant to be kept. That's what Pops taught me," Rook says, watching my face.

I press my eyes closed. "It's still too dangerous. Do you even know what Djinn blood does?" I open my eyes again to find him inches from me, appearing to study my face with his magical vision.

"Very much. It has healing properties for one thing. Did *you* know that?"

I blanch. "I...I... It changes humans into magicians when they ingest it."

Rook cups my cheek in his hand. "I know, Mira. But it also heals human wounds. It's like technology. It isn't the tech that's good or bad. It's what we as people decide to do with it."

I stand there, stunned. I don't know what to say except, "That doesn't change anything. It's the people who make the wrong decisions that I worry about. And what of the Djinn? What if others decide to find one of us and drain her?"

I know my voice trembles with pain and anger, but I cannot help it. All I see is Rhada's beautiful face, empty and swollen after Kitra and her Council were through with her. "They take what doesn't belong to them, and they don't care about the consequences. Then they keep taking because it's never enough!"

I don't realize I've backed into the bed until I find myself sitting and shaking.

Rook approaches slowly, as though I'm a wounded lion. He kneels beside me and places his hands on my knees.

"I want to prevent the type of hurt you've suffered, Mira. I can see it in you. I've seen it with others growing up on the streets, but yours is a special kind of pain that comes from humans' desires for power. I'm giving it to them a bit at a time so they don't take without permission. They won't have the ability to take more than that because they know there are so many others watching. Eventually, I see a world where magic is just part of who we all are, like eye or hair color. Can you see my vision, Mira?"

Hot tears sting my eyes, but I don't stop them from falling onto his hands. This blind man has seen through my carefully crafted shell. "I see it," I admit.

He tightens his hands and smiles.

"But it won't be enough. Djinn will still be more powerful and therefore coveted as servants to the whims of those who crave more."

"There's an answer to that too, but it will take longer to work. Possibly more than a generation." Rook rises to sit beside me on the bed.

"What would that be?"

"Mixing Djinn DNA with human. Eventually there is little difference between the two."

8

WHO AM I?

"That's not possible," I say instantly.

"It's not only possible, it's natural." Rook cups my face in his palm.

"You don't need these with me. I like to see your eyes." I reach up and pull off his sunglasses to set them to the side. Not only is it true that I think his amber eyes are beautiful, but I also need to see them to judge how he really feels. I've found one truth about humans over the last millennium—their eyes don't lie.

Right now, Rook's eyes tell me that he believes in a better world—no, not just believes it. He's seen it.

"Tell me," I whisper, taking his face in my hands and running my thumbs along the rough stubble on his face.

"Humans and Djinn can procreate. It doesn't happen often, and as far as I know, the two have to be in love. I know it doesn't make a lot of sense, but it does happen, which means we can commingle the DNA going forward."

I laugh. I can't help it. I don't mean to belittle his beliefs, but I've never heard such an absurd thing. He stiffens and tries to pull away, and I hold him still, tempering my reaction with a sigh.

"I'm sorry. It's just something that's never even been in my wheelhouse. Tell me, when has this supposedly happened?"

"It's enough to tell you it has. I've seen it. I need you to believe me, Mira, but naming individuals puts them at risk. I want to trust you, but you are part of some organization that wants to destroy everything I've worked for, and I have no doubt you are capable of it if you put your effort into it. You are Djinn, and I know you have others you can combine powers with."

Rook does pull away this time, standing and pacing while visibly attempting to regain control of a temper I have yet to have seen boiling inside him. His aura pulses red and green as though the two are fighting each other for control, but the emerald color washes over him and the red turns back to rust and then to copper before he faces me again, dropping to his knees before me once more.

"Mira, you've trusted me thus far. You've delayed your objective, and I hope it's because somewhere inside you, you see the merits of what I'm doing and that I'm not a danger or a threat to anything or anyone you care about. But it goes both ways. I don't know you any more than you know me. I've tried to give you a peek tonight at who I am and what I stand for. It's all I have. But I have people I love too. People I have to protect."

"You let me meet Pops." Returning his touch takes immense control. All I want is to drop to my own knees and devour his beautiful mouth.

"I'm good at reading people, Mira. And I don't think you'd hurt an innocent man."

No. I would not. Not unless I'm forced to by someone else, and I intend to make sure that never happens again.

"What makes you think I'd hurt this child of Djinn and human?" My voice is small, curious.

Rook shakes his head, taken aback. "I don't think... I mean, I hope you wouldn't. But if you really believe eliminating the Djinn blood on the black market is that dangerous, who's to say you wouldn't try to destroy such a child because of some supposed threat it poses to you? And not just you, Mira, but the Order of which I know nothing about."

I nod, and he stands, offering me a hand.

"There's so much to take in from what you've told me. So much to pull apart and try to understand."

"I still have one more day to convince you. You gave me the week-end." Rook pulls me close, and parts of me come to life in anticipation of a kiss.

"Then we should meet again," I say, cutting him off as he dips his head. Whatever this strong pull or connection is between us, I need to delay it. I have to have a clear head to deal with the information he's given me. But I promise my aching body that when I'm done with business, I will give in to its desires at least for one night. Rook doesn't seem to have any qualms over that.

He nods and steps back. "Tomorrow? Same time?"

"I'll meet you at your place this time," I say with a wink.

When I travel back to my own place and he disappears from view, I let my lungs deflate of air and collapse on my chair. What are the implications of this new information? Would Djinn hybrids pose a threat in some way? Would they too be susceptible to enslavement by others for use of their magic? How often could it happen? And who is the child Rook spoke of?

I attempt to clear my head by taking a walk by the lake. The air is colder than comfortable for most people now that the end of November has taken the last leaves from the trees. So I have the board-walk mostly to myself. The waning moon casts its light over the water, highlighting the ceaseless motion.

I pause, watching the Ferris wheel in the distance. There's something so haunting about a being built for a purpose and remaining empty and unused even if only for the time being. If I'd have asked Kitra, I'm sure she would have been all too happy to tell me my purpose was to service her every whim and desire, to carry her around and around in an unending cycle. Then thoughts of Rhada and our first days together in human skin fill my mind.

We're here to enjoy the pleasures humans take for granted.

That never felt true either and certainly is worthless as a purpose.

This body never felt completely right if I'm honest. It's like a dress I had to put on to fit in, but not one that truly reflects me. What does? I wonder. What is my purpose? Would I be happier on the other side of the veil?

I've tried living that way, the way I was born into existence, but even there I feel as though something is lacking, and at least staying on this side when Leela finally gets her wish and closes the door I will be on the same side as those I care about.

I think of the way Rook sees me, my energy filling this vessel. That's the truest reflection of self I've ever experienced. Can he see what I am really here for?

I shake off such a ridiculous thought. This is not why I'm here. I am here to decide what to do about the black market and the dissemination of Djinn Blood. I believe Rook when he says the blood is willingly taken. I don't think those that belong to the Aladdin would allow any such torture. I wonder briefly if Silas has ever donated his own blood for Rook's cause.

I'll have to tell Dira about this development. No more time should be invested in what is, for all intents and purposes, a dead end. We need to free the final Djinn so that we can close the portal at the allotted time.

No time like the present.

I appear on the doorstep of Dira's small bungalow. The moon is the same here, though lower in the sky as it's technically three hours earlier in this time zone. The California air is warmer but still stings the bare skin of my arms. When I knock, the door swings open for me. It's a polite gesture not to walk into another's home. I won't even do it to Leela or Taj for fear of walking in on something I'd rather not see with their significant others.

I find Dira at her small desk bathed in the glow of her computer screen and the Himalayan salt lamp beside it. She barely looks up.

"Nice outfit."

"Thanks." I conjure a chair and a glass of wine for each of us.

"Did you find anything at Aladdin?" she asks, finally turning away from her screen. If she were human, I'd most certainly find dark circles and lines beneath her large eyes. She shows no such outward signs of stress or fatigue, but her loss of Rachim is still relatively fresh. I know what it is to lose a Djinni lover to murder. She's never had to confide a word.

I fill her in on what I've learned about the black market but hold back details of my attraction to Rook, his personal information and abilities, and the idea of the Djinn hybrids. The more I speak, the more I realize Rook's plans may prove fruitless no matter what if we close the veil and lose the majority of our powers and immortality anyway.

Dira taps her chin with a chewed-up pen before responding. I sip my wine.

"We should wipe it now that you have access."

I set the glass down a bit too hard. "It's a waste of energy. There's no harm in it. Even the DB will lose its potential worth when we close the curtain. We should secure the last six outliers. We only have a few weeks, and we can't afford to lose focus."

Dira laughs nervously. "It takes very little energy or focus to wipe out the threat. It's worth the trouble just in case."

My mouth tightens into a line, my teeth grinding together. "I should check with Taj."

"Then why bother to come here? I thought we were doing this to keep some of the pressure off him." The pen clatters to the desk, and Dira runs her hands down over her tired face.

"No. We're doing this because we both need something to put all our effort into so we don't have to face the reality of life without certain people in it."

The air grows thick and full of static from the power rising between us, though on the surface we remain calm and still. I've dared speak of the unspoken agreement. Perhaps I've realized that it's not helpful to either of us.

"I wish we could bring back those we love," I say softly, reaching for her hand, which she yanks away.

"Not even a dozen Djinn can bring him back." She focuses on her lap, and her voice is thin, even.

She's right. We've tried. We started with the human companion of Leela and Jered. But the closest we could come was summoning his energy from wherever he now resides. Gabe's message was of love and peace, which satisfied them. Curiously, Rhada and the other Djinn could not be summoned in the same way, which made me wonder if we even have souls. Or perhaps we were souls that had destroyed our essence when we dared find our own bodies.

"He would want you to live, Dira. And ultimately that's all Rhada wanted for me. To live and experience the"—I search for a word other than sensuality because that's what she had been so obsessed with—"happiness available to us in human bodies."

It's that simple really. Happiness is the goal, isn't it? And that's the something whose absence I feel so keenly. Rhada equated that with sex, which was new and exciting to her, filled with pleasure. An easy mistake to make, to confuse and conflate the two.

"What would make you happy right now?" I ask her, standing suddenly.

She stares up at me with blank eyes. "Happy?

"What did you like to do before Rachim?"

She blinks as though I'm speaking a foreign language. "I liked to swim in the ocean."

"Come with me," I say, holding out a hand.

"Where are we going?" she asks, joining me.

I smile. "We are going for a midnight swim."

9

IN THE BEGINNING

"Why so glum?" Taj asks, hanging from a branch in the top of the olive tree we meet in. He swings back and forth, the muscles in his arms protruding from the effort.

"Rhada has disappeared. She said she'd be back, but she went off with Kush and some other human two days ago."

"Why not accompany her?" He swings forward, letting go and landing to balance perfectly on top of the branch beside me. It dips and sways slightly under the change in weight, and I fling out a hand to grasp another and steady myself.

"It does not amuse me like it does her."

Taj runs a comforting hand down my arm. When I glance up, his face is sympathetic, and I feel the color rush over my own.

"Have you told her you don't want her to continue?"

"I don't know what I want," I snap. But I do. I want her to be content with only me.

Taj sighs and squeezes my hand. "I suggest you find something else to occupy your time then while you wait. If she says she'll return, she will."

"What about you?" I don't want to dwell on my problems any more than I must.

"I met someone. A peddler from a neighboring town."

"That's lovely," I say, trying to mean it.

"Not really. See, after we shared a night of debauchery, he told me he had a wife and family."

"Oh. What did you do?" I sit down, letting my legs dangle in the air, and he follows suit.

"I turned him into a sidewinder and put a bag of gold and diamonds in his wife's sewing basket."

I laugh.

When Leela pops in to join us, my heart nearly skips a beat, hoping it's Rhada. But the second I see her flushed face, I know it's not.

"He's mine!" she exclaims. "I've finally bedded him, and oh, it was amazing. You should have warned me about the fire danger, Taj!" She slaps his arm playfully.

"Fire danger?" I ask.

Leela giggles and spins in midair before landing and sitting between us. At least someone is happy with their counterpart out here.

"Achan and I will be so happy wandering the wilderness."

"I should go." I stand abruptly, not wishing to hear any more about her good fortune.

"What's the hurry?" she asks, widening those big, innocent eyes of hers.

"I have things to experiment with." I nod to Taj, and he grins before I leave.

I pace the length of our empty home as I search my mind for something I'd like to do besides be with Rhada. I enjoy the market, I decide, coming up disturbingly short on other possibilities. So with a sigh, I pop over to the bustling area, inhaling the delightful aroma of tea and incense.

"Jewels for a beautiful lady?" suggests a raspy voice to my left. I approach the old woman's cart and smile.

"What catches your eye, my dear?" she asks. I'm hypnotized by the deep wrinkles in her skin and the warm smile on her face.

I peer at the table of wares, and a carved and polished ruby glows scarlet in the dwindling sunlight. It throws dancing embers across the table and the other beads and jewels there. It doesn't seem to belong.

"She's beautiful, isn't she?" the woman says.

I'd almost forgotten she was there. I nod.

"It would make a beautiful ring."

I think of Rhada, and an idea takes form. Perhaps a gift to bind us together? Something symbolic of our love and commitment. "Her favorite color is red," I mumble.

"I love red as well," a girl says from beside me.

I glance at the beautiful young woman I'd met my first day in a human body. Sakhr's daughter. "Kitra, isn't it?" I ask.

"Yes. And you are Mira. Rhada has told me so much about you." She offers her hand, and I take it. Her skin is smooth and tender, her nails carefully manicured as though she hasn't worked a day in her life.

"You know her?" I ask, unable to keep the surprise from my voice.

"Well."

The way she says it, with a knowing smile, makes me withdraw my hand.

"This piece is red as well," the peddler says, redirecting my attention to a large, oval-shaped fire opal that gleams when she holds it to the light. "Or if you like something less ostentatious..." She fingers a rounded tiger's eye stone striped brown and black, already set inside a silver setting.

"I'll take all three," Kitra says in a commanding tone. "I like to collect beautiful things, Mira. Don't you?"

The woman perks up and busies herself wrapping the jewels for her. My heartbeat quickens when the ruby disappears into the packaging. I still need something for Rhada.

"I don't collect anything," I answer.

"You should start. It's something fun to do and something men can't do anything about." She rolls her eyes back on the word "men" and grins.

"Your father, Sakhr, he's very controlling?" I ask as I peruse the other wares on the table.

"Just like all men. They think with their penises and assume they are smarter than us. Fools. We don't even need them to survive unless we care to procreate. I'm never making that mistake. I will give no man a reason to control me again."

"You shouldn't speak ill of your father, miss." The old woman shoves the package at her, tied with string. Kitra grimaces and hands over a fistful of coin.

"I'd kill the bastard if I could," she says, taking my hand and leading me away from the table. "I'm so glad I ran into you, Mira. Come back with me to my house. I'll show you my collections. I've been terribly bored today."

"I don't know..."

"Don't worry!" She laughs. "Sakhr is out of town. Probably with another whore."

Rhada is nowhere to be found. Why not?

I agree and follow her to her home on the top of the hill.

10

A TALK WITH TAJ

THE MIDNIGHT SWIM IN THE PACIFIC PROVES BOTH INVIGORATING AND THE perfect release. By the time I am finished, my muscles ache with the kind of well-earned strain I feel after an adrenaline-releasing workout. It seems to have done the trick for Dira as well based on her lazy smile as she leans back on the sand, staring up at the stars.

"Thank you, Mir. I needed this."

"We should do it more often," I say, conjuring a towel and rubbing at my wet hair. "Will you be okay if I leave you now? I have something I must see to."

"Of course." Dira smiles at me, and some of the glow is back in her eyes.

With renewed purpose, I appear outside Taj and Cal's apartment where I ring the bell.

A minute later, a bleary-eyed Cal opens the door, bare-chested with striped, low-hanging pajama pants.

"It's for you, Taj. I win," he calls over his shoulder before stepping aside to let me in.

I change out of my bathing suit and into a simple blue sundress and flip-flops, still feeling the California vibes. "What did you win?" I ask in a whisper. The two of them constantly bet each other over ridiculous things. It's become quite the source of entertainment.

Cal wiggles his eyebrows. "I get to decide what we do tomorrow night."

I smile, knowing he means more than just picking a venue for their date.

"So it's your fault I'm going to have to wear heels tomorrow, is it?" Taj asks, appearing in the doorway to the bedroom, arms folded across his chest. He wears a pair of black silk boxers.

"No. It's yours for making the bet," I correct him as I plant a peck on his cheek.

"Well, good night, you two. I'm going to get some beauty rest so I'm completely refreshed for tomorrow night." Cal tousles my hair and smacks Taj's ass on his way back in the bedroom. The door closes after him, muffling the song he whistles as he goes.

"So to what do I owe this four o'clock in the morning visit?" Taj asks, popping over to the leather sectional.

I join him and lick my lips, deciding where to begin.

"Ah. Speechless. Looks like we need a drink." Taj snaps, and we each hold a martini glass with four olives. He then leans back and sucks one off the tip of his plastic pick.

I set my glass on the table and take a breath. "I met someone."

Taj nearly chokes on his martini.

"He's a magician from the club the other night," I confess.

"But?" he asks, setting his own glass down and eyeing me suspiciously.

"But it's complicated." I can't bring myself to say much more as I shift my position on the seat.

"I see. Isn't it always?" he muses. "Is that why you're here?"

Was it?

"Have you ever heard of a magician who was more powerful than Kitra?" I blurt out.

Taj spits out the sip he's taking and sets his glass down again.

"Powerful in what sense?" he asks, eyes narrowing.

I shift again and take a sip of my own drink as I think it over. "As in speed and ability to counter Djinn magic or blinking to new locations. Maybe even reading thoughts?"

Taj straightens to the point I suspect someone has shoved a rod down his spine. He takes my drink from my hand, and it disappears while his eyes throw emerald sparks.

"Who?" he asks.

I don't like his reaction. What if he plans to kill Rook if I out him?

He sees my hesitation and takes my face in his hand. His eyes soften with affection. "I'm sorry about my reaction. I trust you, Mir."

"Trust *me*?" I blurt. "I was worried you meant to incinerate the threat, and I happen to be rather fond of him."

Taj laughs, his chest shaking with it. "It appears we both mean to protect someone."

"Does Jered have such ability?" I guess.

Taj laughs again. "No. He's quite formidable, I admit, but it's his younger sister, my former master, that I mean to protect."

"Sophie?" The world spins, and I clutch the arm of the sofa. "She does all that? Why in the universe haven't you said anything?"

"The same reason you hesitated to give up a name I suspect. I will die to protect her. I proved that a year ago when I defied a command to murder her. I have a short list of those I love, though it seems to grow larger by the moment since I've been freed."

I nod, taking this in. Of course Taj loves the child who freed him. So it isn't unheard of for a magician to possess these powers. Perhaps it's something about the new generation of magicians that allows this evolution. Perhaps no DNA tampering is even necessary. I smile inwardly and wonder if their powers will also dampen when we shut the door.

"Mira, you cannot share this information with others. I don't want anyone threatening Sophie."

"Of course not," I agree. I wish no harm to the child. I certainly wish no harm to Rook.

Taj yawns, stretching his arms into the air and making a ghastly sound that makes me laugh again. A hint that it's late, but I have another question now.

"Before I go, I need to know something. Do you really believe closing the veil is the right thing to do? Do we really understand enough?"

Taj drops his hands and downs his drink. "I don't know. Lee is adamant."

"But what if she's wrong? What if it doesn't work? Or..." I pause, uncomfortable about giving voice to the idea that's been tickling the back of my mind. "Or we disappear altogether? Like Rhada and Rachim," I finish in a whisper, unable to look at him. Facing the idea that there is no other existence beyond this for us is too difficult for me.

Taj pulls me into a much-needed embrace, and I rest my head on his shoulder. He always did smell of cinnamon, and that familiar scent comforts me now. "You know what I believe?"

"What?" I prompt.

"That the only reason we were unable to contact them is that the universe knows even Djinn powers must be limited."

"But Gabe—"

"Was a human. And therefore a different matter entirely."

I inhale deeply and let the breath out slowly before sitting up and wiping at my eyes. "Thank you, Taj."

"Anytime." He stands as I do, and I lean in to press a kiss to his cheek before leaving. My last visual is of him touching a hand to the spot and smiling.

When I arrive home, I turn on my cell phone to find ten calls from Leela. Why she bothers with human communication, I have no idea. I barely use the device and constantly forget I even have it.

I dial her back and sink into my oversized armchair.

"Where have you been?" she demands in place of a greeting.

"Out. What's the emergency?"

"We have an exact date and time for the ceremony. We can close the veil on December eighth at 11:11 p.m."

I swallow.

"Mira?"

"That's a week and a half from now," I say, moving over to my makeshift office and firing up my computer screen. "We have six Djinn to free."

"Five. I already took care of my new assignment."

I frown. "I don't want you or anyone else rushing into these things without following procedure. It can be dangerous."

"Yes, Mother. But it's done, and now we're down to five. Give one to Taj, one to Cal, one to you, one to Dira, and one to myself, and it can be done by the end of the week. Aren't you excited?"

"No." I don't mean to hurt her. But it's the truth. "I'm sorry, Lee. I...I guess I feel like there are too many unknowns. It feels so sudden."

This time, she's the silent one. I wait, pressing my eyes closed and hoping she understands. That she hears me.

"Everyone else has agreed," she says, finally, voice thick with emotion. "I want you to be with us, but if you have to cross back over..."

"No. I'm staying. Either way, I'm staying. I just think we should do more research before—"

"We need this now, Mir. I need this. I can't live jumping at shadows anymore. Hold on."

I pull the phone from my face just as Leela appears in my living room. Her skin is streaked with tear tracks, and she looks rather pale, twisting her hands together in worry.

"What is it?" I sense something bigger is happening here.

"You can't tell Jered. Or Taj," she says, grabbing my arms to look me in the face.

"What is it?" I repeat. My pulse races as I take in her appearance as a whole, far more bedraggled than normal for her or any Djinni.

"Something's wrong with me. It started a few weeks ago. I noticed I was tired."

I wrinkle my brow. "That's a human thing."

"Exactly. And it gets stranger. I've also been having dizzy spells and stomach pains."

"Why don't you want to tell anyone? We should all try to figure this out. Lee, this could be serious. Djinn don't get sick." I guide her over to the sofa, and we sit.

"I don't want to scare them. Whatever it is, it's only more of a reason to go through with closing the veil. I can't explain it, but I have a strong feeling it will cease when that happens."

I draw in a sharp breath through my nose. No part of that is logical, but what else is new when it comes to Leela?

"Please, Mir. You don't have to help, but please let me have this."

I look into her sunken eyes as she grasps my arm so hard that her nails draw drops of blood.

"I'll stay out of it."

It's one less thing I have to agonize over.

11

A DATE IN PARIS

I SPEND THE DAY PLANNING THE RESCUE OF THE FINAL FIVE AS I'VE DUBBED them. Throwing myself into work is the best way I have of dealing with Leela's predicament and stubborn refusal to tell the others. Three are assigned by the time I pause to prepare for my date with Rook.

A smile spreads over my face when I realize I've labeled it a date in my mind.

I decide to go with a corset-style top and flowy skirt that skims the middle of my thighs. Both are decorated with tiny roses. I pull my hair up into a twist and add some light makeup. A pair of strappy tan sandals, and I'm pleased with the result.

When I appear outside Aladdin, Tyrannus leans against the wall in the spot I first saw Rook. He nods as I pass by and into the club. The loud thrum of the music blasts me along with a burst of air conditioning. The club is still about half empty because of the early hour, and I notice Amy behind the bar mixing drinks in a tornado of practiced movement. I wave, and she waves back.

Feeling far more at ease in the space than I did that first night, I saunter over to the winding metal stairs and pass through the rope on my way up. I'm about to knock on the door to his apartment when Rook swings it open and greets me without sunglasses.

His amber eyes are as beautiful as ever, and I can't keep the stupid grin off my face. I have to admit I'm glad he can't see it. The rest of him looks just as delicious. He wears a white band tee that hugs his muscles and sets off the bronzed skin next to it. His jeans are tight like the other night and ripped in strategic places that make me want to dig my fingers in and finish pulling them off.

"Right on time," he says, stepping aside so I can enter.

He shuts the door behind me and turns. I'm on him in the space of a heartbeat, bodies melding together and tongues enjoying a dance that feels both practiced and new. He lifts me, and I hug his hips with my legs, tangling my hands in his long mane of silken hair.

He turns, and I'm pressed back to the door, neither of us coming up for air as he slides his hands beneath me to cup my ass, fingers dancing further between my legs. A rumble erupts from my throat as he connects with the part of me that's dripping with anticipation.

He detaches his mouth from mine as I throw my head back into the door, and he nibbles his way down my neck and to my chest.

"We should talk." I force the words out between ragged breaths, already full of regret for interrupting the things he's doing to me.

He pauses, fingers retracting, head pressed between my breasts, so close to being released from my carefully chosen top. "Give me a minute."

I try to stay still as we both recover, and he lets me slide slowly back down to the ground.

"You're killing me on purpose, aren't you?" he asks, stalking toward his kitchen to retrieve two bottles of water.

I accept one tossed to me and watch him guzzle his down, Adam's apple bobbing as he swallows.

"Obviously I'm just as distracted as you are. But we have some things to discuss. I've decided to allow your computer program to run undisturbed. But I want something in return."

Rook raises an eyebrow and sets his empty bottle down on the counter.

"I want in. I want to know what's happening and who's buying. That way there won't be any unapproved surprises from someone with less altruistic intentions than you."

"I like to keep things private for my clients." He crosses his arms, and every muscle in his broad chest, shoulders, and arms clenches. So do my thighs.

"Fine. It can be private between them and us."

"So there's an *us* now?" he asks.

"Do you have a problem with that?"

"I don't know. I've always been a private person. I really don't discuss my business with anyone. No offense to you, Mira, but you walked into my life a few days ago, and since then, everything's been turned upside down."

I nod, unable to find the words. I was assuming he feels the same as I do. Clearly, I'm incorrect. But this isn't about us. This is about potential danger to other Djinn, and my job comes first.

"Those are my terms. I can destroy it instead, if you prefer." I stalk my way over to where he stands and set my bottle of water down hard on the counter by his.

He stares at me with citrine eyes, and I know he's reading my energy and my thoughts. There's no hiding my feelings from this man, and that makes me want to walk back out the door. But I stand my ground. For the Order. For Taj and Leela and Dira and Cal and all the others I am sworn to protect.

There will be no more Rhadas or Rachims on my watch.

"You are so damn sexy, it's hard to think," Rook says. "Are you distracting me on purpose?"

"Maybe." I hop up onto the counter and cross my legs.

"I suppose I can work with your offer. I was going to take you with me on a transaction tonight so you could see how it works and that nothing is amiss."

"Sounds fun. What's the plan?" I cock my head and realize my hair is a mess from my entrance. So I blink, and it falls in loose ripples over my shoulders.

"We have a meeting in Paris on Avenue des Champs-Élysées in

twenty minutes. We are meeting at an outside café and delivering a vial of DB to a buyer. Their code name is Daffodil."

I snort. "Daffodil? Doesn't sound so scary."

"It isn't meant to. Just private to protect real names and identities. My code name is Raven."

"Not so far off from Rook." I slip my hands over his shoulders and pull him close. "Twenty minutes? That's all we had and you thought we could finish what we started?"

The corner of his mouth crooks upward. "Somehow, I don't think what we started will ever be finished, and that's what I can't wrap my brain around. You weren't in my life plans, Mira."

"Sometimes the plans we make aren't what's best for us."

"Are you saying you are what's best for me?"

His scent is intoxicating. "I might be too biased to answer that."

"Let's go to Paris." He offers me a hand, and his sunglasses appear on his face. "I like to be at these meetings early and check out the surroundings."

I leap off the counter to join him. "So you do know that not everyone's motives are pure. I'm so proud."

He glares right through his shades and pulls me along to Paris. To my surprise, the café still bustles with activity at one in the morning. I scan the street and the inside of the two-story building when we enter to claim a seat. We hold hands and ask for a table outside on the walkway. The hostess is perturbed, chattering about it being too chilly as I don't have a jacket. But we insist, and she shrugs, showing us outside to a round corner table overlooking the sights and sounds of the Paris nightlife. The Arc de Triomphe glows golden in the night at the end of the avenue where pedestrians meander hand in hand. The pavement is wet, and the many lights reflect upward as though the whole scene is caught in the midst of a galaxy of stars.

"It is beautiful. Though as I recall, the scenes depicted on the Arc were less victorious and bloodier in reality. I suppose it's all the perspective. They say history is told by the victors."

Rook peruses the menu, or he pretends to. "You were there?"

I shrug and order a glass of white wine for each of us, holding up two fingers to the server from a distance. "*Deux verres de chardonnay, s'il vous plaît.*"

"I don't drink when I'm working." Rook sets the menu down.

"Suit yourself. I'll have both. So what does Daffodil look like? And do you have the vial? I didn't even see you get it. Where do you keep them anyway?" I strain my neck, turning every which way in search of anyone with a magician's aura. Several line the street, including one bicyclist that zooms by. A suspicious time to cycle in my opinion.

"Mira." Rook's hand on my own draws my concentration back, and I find him chuckling slightly. "Relax. This isn't a drug deal, at least not in the way you're picturing. I have the vial. I transported it into my pocket before we left. I keep them in a safe in my apartment."

"How long do they stay fresh?" I ask, curious.

"Indefinitely with magic."

The server brings our wine, and I request a plate of appetizers as well. May as well enjoy ourselves.

Rook smiles and rises from the table, glancing over my shoulder.

The wine nearly swooshes over the lips of the glasses as I stand abruptly to join him. An elderly woman hobbles through the gate. She's a magician, judging by the splash of green and sunny yellow that surrounds her. I suppose she wants an easy way to share the power with a loved one.

"You must be Raven," she says, smiling at Rook, who holds out a hand to shake.

"And you are Daffodil," I say, not extending my own hand.

She nods and coughs before replying. "My favorite flower. Oh my. Are you Djinn?" The color floods from her pale face, and she nearly stumbles taking a step back.

"There's nothing to be afraid of," Rook assures her, reaching to steady her and pulling out a chair so she can settle off her unreliable feet. She doesn't take her eyes off me. I recognize the true fear that resides there. It was the way many looked at me when I was under Kitra's control. I don't like it. I never have.

I take a gulp of wine and offer her the other glass.

"I'm sorry," she says. "It's been a long time since I've seen one of you, and the stories, you know. Tricksters they say, or worse. Unpredictable."

"I suppose unpredictable is true enough," I say with what I hope is a comforting smile. "I mean you no harm. I would only do so if I thought you were a threat to myself or anyone else." The jury is still out on that particular issue, though it's comforting to hear she's run into my kind before and lived.

She seems to steel herself and make up her mind about something. Then she sets her bag on the table in front of her. "I don't want to keep either of you. It was very kind of you to meet me here."

"So you are quite adept with technology," I say, finishing off my glass.

She startles a bit, and I grin.

"No offense, but most people of your generation don't know their way around a computer, let alone how to get on a magic server without some technical knowledge."

I can feel Rook tense from here, but I ignore him. Surely, he sees a disconnect.

"Oh. Well, yes. It was my grandson Devon that helped me find you. He let me pick the name of course. He's a young human boy. I'm doing this for him."

"Doing what exactly?" I press, leaning forward so she can see my eyes clearly.

"Mira," Rook warns.

"I don't mind explaining it," Daffodil says quickly, waving a dismissive hand at him.

I sit back, triumphant, and refill my glass with magic. Is she going to tell us that he wants to be stronger? That she wants her grandson to be able to do what she does and carry on the family tradition?

"Devon, he has a condition. It's cancer. He's only fourteen, and we've tried to help, my daughter and I, but I guess magic can only do so much. Devon did some of his own research. He loves using the magical web, and his mother helps him get started. Anyway, he found that Djinn blood could possibly help him. I'd do anything for Devon. I'd be forever in your debt, Mira. Whatever you require of me. Lord knows it's not money."

The woman looks me in the eye despite trembling in terror. I'm speechless. Does she expect me to ask her to be my slave in exchange for helping her grandson?

"I don't know if Djinn blood will solve the problem," I say in way of answer.

"It's been shown to be seventy-six percent effective against cancer growth." Rook's voice is soft.

"I'd do it if it were only a five percent chance," she says, tears brimming in her eyes.

Rook slides his hand over toward hers, and when he lifts it, a small test tube filled with blood is left on the tablecloth.

Daffodil gasps and takes the vial in her trembling hand, handling it with such a delicate and slow touch that I sit mesmerized as she places it securely in her bag.

"Now what is your price?" she asks, eyes closed to steady herself.

"Knowing we've done all we can for your grandson," Rook says with a genuine smile.

Daffodil startles and whimpers slightly. Tears finally overflow from where they've collected in her eyelids. "Oh, thank you. God bless you both."

Rook stands to assist her with her chair as she leaves through the gate she came in. Our calamari arrives moments after, and when the server turns away, I'm left staring at the man on the other side of the table.

"I didn't know our blood heals like that." The statement is an admission of an embarrassing truth. How is it in a thousand years I hadn't realized the effects of my own blood? I suppose Kitra never had need of helping another of her own kind.

"It mutates human cells," Rook explains in his soft voice.

"But magicians don't get stronger the more they take. Are you sure it will help him?" I lean forward as though the table between us is an inconvenience.

"No. I'm not sure. But it has helped others in similar situations. I think that magic is perhaps a finite thing for individuals, but correcting health is something different. It's all I can really say. I'd love to find someone trustworthy, willing, and able to do the research."

I nod as my gaze falls to the table. Rook reaches for a piece of calamari, and as he dips it in sauce, I notice a small bruise on the inside of his arm, a tiny red dot marking the center of the faded purplish circle, the size of a dime.

"How much Djinn blood do you have in your safe?" I ask as he chews.

"Maybe five vials at a time."

"I see," I say, catching his eyes behind his sunglasses, "and how often do you draw your own blood?"

12

IN THE BEGINNING

KITRA'S HOME IS LAVISH, FAR MORE SO THAN OURS, WITH WINDING HALLWAYS *and rooms galore. She leads me with purpose down one hall and into her own rooms. The decorations here contrast with the rest of the house I've seen. They are gold and red. Satin sheets and round pillows decorate the large bed, and huge mirrors adorns an entire wall.*

"Is it mirrors you collect?" I ask, watching as many Kitras and Miras stand in the room.

She laughs throwing her head back like it's the funniest thing she's ever heard. "No! But it's not a bad idea. I collect unique things like jewels and magic."

"Magic?" I ask, taken aback. I thought humans knew of no such thing.

"There is more to this world than meets the eye." She runs a finger down the length of my arm, eliciting a shiver and warmth that spreads between my legs. This body is so sensitive. It irks me that it responds to the touch of others besides my beloved Rhada despite the fact that she has no such reservations.

"Show me your jewels," I say, wishing to distract her.

She smiles and leads me over to a cedar box with ornate carvings of geometric shapes on the top. I notice an eye in the center. When she lifts the lid, I peer inside. Half of the velvet surface is taken by an array of gems like the ones she now unwraps from the market and lays in open spaces between others. The other side of the trunk is filled with more haphazard-looking objects including a dagger with dried blood on its edge and half-burned candles.

"What are those?" I ask, pointing to them.

"Those are the items I collect tied to magic." She shuts the lid carefully and locks it before leading me over to sit on the edge of her bed.

"Tell me, Mira, are you and Rhada related?" She walks to a thin table lining her wall, and I wait, curious until she appears with two glasses of a glowing bronze liquid, handing one to me and sipping on the other.

"No. We are lovers," I say, seeing no reason to hide my feelings.

Kitra nearly spits out her drink. I sip mine, appreciating the strong yet sweet aroma and warmth as it travels down my throat.

"You shouldn't announce that to just anyone around here," Kitra says.

I nod and take a larger swig of my drink. My mind softens like a cloud has settled inside it. "But it does not bother you?"

She takes another sip of her own drink, and I copy her, draining the glass and licking my lips to make sure I take in every bit of the precious liquid.

"Bother me? I enjoy pleasures of the flesh as well." She scoots beside me, and before I realize what's happening, her lips are on mine, her tongue licking off whatever stray drops I may I have missed.

I want to explain to her that though I am flattered, it is only Rhada that I wish to be with from now on, but I can't seem to get the words out. And when I part my mouth to speak, she darts her tongue inside to fill the space. She lays me back on the bed, and I feel as though I am floating as the room spins around us. I do not like the feeling of being unable to grasp where I am in relation to anything but this strange girl.

She caresses my breast and strokes my nipple, which has somehow come loose from the fabric of my dress. She pinches it between her fingers, rolling it as I try to gasp for air.

She pulls back and laughs again. The sound echoes strangely around me as everything continues to spin. "I like to experiment," she says from somewhere far away.

I try to lift my body, my head, any part of me, but I seem to have no control.

"I added a potion I bought off a witch to your drink."

My dress is being slid off me. Hands trail up my legs, and my knees lift, supported by Kitra's shoulders.

"You should be honored I chose to waste it on you. I'm not sure if it's magic exactly, but you won't remember most of this. I just want to try a few things you may not have agreed to otherwise."

I wake with a start, sitting up in the foreign bed, naked beside Kitra, sleeping soundly. I nearly double over as pain grips my lower abdomen and shoots between my legs. Vague images of candles dripping wax and unforgiving objects inside me make me lean over the edge of the bed and vomit.

When the racking of my body subsides, I wipe the tears from my eyes and search for my garments. Kitra stretches and sits lazily up on the bed.

"Leaving so soon?" she asks. "Maybe next time Rhada visits, you can come over and we can have some fun together, Mira who is not Rhada's sister but her lover."

I pull the dress over myself in haste and find all words have dried up on my tongue. I should do what Taj does and turn her into a sidewinder. She wants to see magic? I'll show her magic.

But the voice of Sakhr from the hall distracts me, and Kitra's face falls, her mask of lust turning to one of fear.

"Where is that lazy she-devil?"

"Hide," she commands. "He will kill us both if he finds another woman here." Not liking what I see in her face, I dive down beside the bed as the door bursts open.

"Naked like the whore you are," Sakhr spits. I cringe as I hear the slap of skin against skin.

"You hiding another one of your lovers in here, Kitra? Not another shepherd boy, I hope. At least bed someone wealthy." More harsh sounds of what I assume is the back of his hand.

"Might as well practice on my cock if you like to suck them so much."

I've heard enough. I disappear along with the vomit on the floor and one more treasure tucked in my pocket from Kitra's collection. She'll never miss it.

13

MAKING LOVE

Rook freezes, calamari halfway to his open mouth.

"How did you know?" he asks, setting it back down again on the plate.

"I can see the mark on your arm. You are stronger and faster than any other magician I've ever known. You told me yourself about Djinn hybrids, or it never would have occurred to me."

"We should go home," he says, and I cannot read his expression.

We travel to his apartment at the top of the stairs inside the Aladdin where he sits at a small table, drumming his fingers on the wood veneer.

I sit on top of said table.

"Why did you not tell me?" I ask.

"You may have wanted to kill me." He tilts his head up plainly, his sunglasses gone again.

He isn't wrong to think that.

"You may still want to, for all I know."

I wince as the pain of his words jolt through my chest. "I'm not going to kill you, Rook."

He nods and pulls his hands through his beautiful hair.

"Will the blood work as well if it is diluted with human DNA?" I ask.

"Humans aren't lesser creatures you know, Mira."

"I did not mean it that way. I just want to be sure it works. For Daffodil and her grandson. If not, I..." I pause, opening my arm to reveal the tender flesh inside the crease at my elbow.

Rook grips my arm on the table, and I turn to him.

"You'd do that? To save him?"

I nod. "Of course I would. I'd donate all of it if it would erase the horrible things I've been forced to do in my miserable life."

"How old are you?" he asks, and the gentleness in his tone suddenly feels wrong, like he's mocking me. But I don't pull away from his touch. I crave it.

"In human terms? I don't know. Well over a thousand."

"How much of that life has been lived free of a master?" His amber eyes hold me there like glistening pots of honey, easing the pain of the answer.

"A few meager years." I whisper the words, afraid I will scare him away, thinking me so broken that I am beyond repair. Perhaps I am.

Instead of running, Rook stands suddenly, his chair scraping against the floor. He pulls on my arm, guiding me off the table and into his embrace where he mashes his mouth against mine, hungry and filled with an emotion I cannot put a name to, but it takes my breath away.

We devour each other right there in the middle of his small kitchen, searching and exploring, needing to know each other in the most intimate way possible. I jump, and he catches me as though we've rehearsed it. He sets me on the edge of the counter, running his hands up my sides until he's released my breasts from the prison of my corset. I moan as he takes first one nipple into his mouth, teasing and coercing it into a hardened nub before moving to the other.

I'm drunk with need as he takes the time to physically remove my clothing, bit by bit, focusing his attentions on each portion of skin he exposes. When he tugs off my underwear, I slide off the counter and rip at his shirt, popping the row of buttons to uncover his chiseled physique beneath. I run my thumbs over his nipples and trace my way down to his waist where I wrench off his pants and boxers in one rough movement.

We stand naked before each other. Our rapid breathing fills the space between us. Then I lunge for him, pulling his mouth to mine with a desperation I've never felt. I wrap my legs around him, but he stops me before I can claim him.

"Mira, wait," he begs, and I hold.

He carries me like that to his bedroom, kicking in the door and laying me across the down comforter so that he hovers above me. I wait, wondering what I've done. If he's decided I am too much baggage.

"In those few years"—he swipes some of my hair to the side gently —"did you have the opportunity to make love?"

I blink, trying to digest his question.

"I'm not a virgin, Rook."

He grins in a way that sends heat right between my legs. "I don't doubt that. What I mean is not sex, but love. Have you...ever had a partner who put your needs first?"

"I've had orgasms," I say, still slightly confused.

He sighs and tries again. "But were those orgasms given to you as a gift because your partner wanted only for you to experience pleasure, not because of their own needs?"

I think about Rhada and when she introduced me to pleasure. Yes, she brought me to orgasm. Yes, she enjoyed doing that. But it wasn't given freely. It was almost as though she took her own pleasure in seeing me unravel. She liked to experiment sexually like Kitra did, and for the first time, I see the similarities in the two of them. I can't stop my heart from racing. Can't catch my breath. I cling to Rook, but I see only Rhada laughing and Kitra with the ruby. I hear her whisper in my ear. *"See Rhada's body on the wall?"*

She played with fire.

"Mira? Are you okay? Breathe." Rook's voice brings me back from where I was. I loved her. Or...I thought that was love. But she was too fond of playing to really want that.

When I come to, I'm sobbing hysterically, cradled naked against

Rook's strong body as he shushes softly in my hair. "That's right, baby. Just slow, deep breaths."

I gasp as the last of my sobs abate and awareness takes over along with something like shame. But Rook won't accept that. He continues to rock me gently back and forth, stroking me, and I settle against him, giving up the tension and the fight. I've fought for too long. It's nice just to be held like this.

When I quiet completely, he peers down at me, his eyes like liquid metal in some long-ago forge.

"Thank you."

He smiles. "Any time. I'm sorry if I triggered something. I shouldn't have pressed you like that. I want you to know that when we're together, for me, it's making love. I don't just fuck around, and I guess I wanted to make sure you had the experience so you know what the difference is."

I swallow the lump in my throat. What if what happens with Rook means Rhada never truly loved me? I need to know. "I'd like you to show me the difference if you're still in the mood."

Rook lays me back on the bed once again, every movement careful and fluid as he kisses me tenderly yet deeply, sweeping his tongue along mine in a dance. He caresses my body, hands flowing along my face, breasts, stomach, and thigh where he shifts along to the sensitive inside skin, awakening my arousal. His fingers meet with hot moisture as he slides them along the folds between my legs and groans at the feel of me, ready for him.

But he doesn't enter me. Instead, he trails a path down my body with his mouth, much as he did with his hands, until he rests between my legs and laps at the same area, slowly dragging his tongue along my entrance and dipping inside.

My hips lift from the bed in an effort to gain more pressure, and he grabs me from underneath, holding me at the right angle so that he can explore more of me. I grip the blankets beneath me in my hands, unable to hold back the moans he draws from deep inside me. His undivided attention turns to my clitoris where he sucks, nips, and licks until I'm in a frenzied state. He slides one hand up to join his mouth, and first one, then two fingers enter me, reaching far inside as they glide in and out in a perfect rhythm.

"Take your time," he says against me and continues his undivided attentions until my release bursts through my shuddering body, and he holds me there, drawing every last bit of mind-shattering orgasm from me and my body has turned to liquid in his hands.

"You taste amazing," he says as he slides back up the bed to join me, his hand causing another involuntary shudder as he places it across my stomach.

"Mmmm," is all I can manage as I roll into him, hand reaching languidly for his cock.

But he stops me. "I'm not done yet."

"I didn't think you were," I say with a laugh.

"I mean I'm not done with you yet." And he sets his practiced mouth and hands to my breasts, twisting and pulling at my nipples until my hips rise from the bed, once again filled with need. He slips his hand below and this time circles my clit with his thumb, pressing and rubbing until I call out once again.

"I want that cock inside me," I almost yell.

And he finally complies, placing himself over me and slipping inside my hungry body until his length hits the magic spot that sends me into overdrive. He fills me like no other man ever has as he buries himself in me. He pulls away, and I groan until he slides back in, repeating his motions until the entire bed bounces and creaks with our movements, pressing into my body as far and hard as he can. I lose control of myself and shatter as fireworks explode all around us. Only then does Rook allow his own release and roll beside me onto the bed.

He waves an arm, and the tiny fires in his ceiling and walls snuff themselves out. I stretch like a cat, completely satisfied.

"So?" he asks, leaning up on his elbow and drawing a lazy circle on my chest.

"So what's the difference?" I tease, but I'm pretty sure my face is glowing.

"Who was he?" he asks.

"She. Well, there was a he as well for a short time at Kitra's palace.

When she found out, she made me turn him to stone. I released him about a year ago."

"You aren't together?" Rook seems more concerned for me than our potential relationship.

"Obviously not. I sent him away to live a new life without the pain of the past. It's what I'd want if I had the option." I shrug and begin tracing my own lines up and down his arms.

"And the she?" he presses.

I sigh. "Her name was Rhada. She was Djinn and the first to die. Do you feel it like we do? When a Djinni is killed?" I turn onto my side, head propped as well.

"Maybe a little. Like a stomachache."

I nod, thinking. "She loved me in her own way. But it wasn't a healthy relationship. I was too blinded by the pain and unfairness of the magician that did it and took myself and my friends as slaves to see past to the reality. I've mourned her for a millennium as the love of my life."

"When maybe there's someone else?" Rook asks, flicking my nipple.

I bat his hand away and frown. "Maybe. We'll see. But I certainly enjoyed making love. You really took your time taking care of my needs."

"Because your pleasure is important to me, Mira." His husky voice wraps me in a cloud of rising want as he strokes my hair back from my face.

"I believe I'll give that a try on you too," I say, sucking in my bottom lip in anticipation of more to come. I can't believe this beautiful being exists. I can't believe this beautiful being could be mine.

I toss the covers over my head and duck down to where his erection is starting to rise again. I help it along with my mouth and tongue until I can barely fit it down my throat.

"You don't have to do this," he says from above in staggered words between gasps of pleasure.

I know I don't. But it's like he said—it makes me happy to do this for him.

When I taste the saltiness of his precum, I lift the curtain of covers and release some of the heat before climbing over him.

"Wait," he says, grasping my hips as I slide my slickness over the length of his cock. "What about you?"

"Oh, believe me, I'm going to come hard, buddy." I place a hand on his chest and begin riding him, this time completely in control.

"Mira." He grunts my name as I continue to work him with my body. The way he's losing control lends steam to my own pleasure, and I hit him where I need to, knowing it's perfect for us both. It doesn't take long for either of us to climax, and I continue gliding my hips over him slowly as I feel him twitch inside me.

"My gods, Mira," he whispers, head pressed into the pillow, eyes closed in ecstasy.

Pleased, I climb off him and lie beside him once again, thinking lazily of days in bed to come.

But as I allow myself to drift into reverie, reality hits me hard.

"Do you know of any other hybrids out there?" I ask, staring at the burn mark in the ceiling above me.

"Maybe one other in passing. As I said, it doesn't happen often, and in her case, the parents were in love as well. It's the only common denominator I can think of."

I tick off the list in my head. Hybrids have a magician's aura. They do not have unnaturally green eyes. They are able to do things other magicians cannot, like move through space and slow time. Read the thoughts of some people.

"You know of someone else?" Rook sits suddenly, his face appearing above me, creased with concern.

Damn his telepathy. "Yes. I think I may. But it doesn't make sense. Her father and mother were most definitely not in love, and neither were Djinn. Yet she is like you."

"Are her parents still around?"

I sit up against the headboard and contemplate Rook's beautiful features. "Her mother is. Perhaps she and I will have a chat."

14

SOPHIE'S STORY

I KNOW WHAT SOPHIE MEANS TO TAJ, SO I DON'T WANT TO ALARM HIM unnecessarily. I decide to talk to her mother, Elle, alone the next morning since the last thing I need is Taj blowing his lid.

I appear before the large suburban house, aware that the only people inside are Elle and Sophie, the latter of whom is in her bedroom upstairs. At the age of ten, her magician's aura is prominent and filled with beautiful colors that could mesmerize for hours. Her mother has no such aura.

Knocking on the door wastes my time, but I will do this as innocuously as possible for Taj's sake.

When Elle opens the door, I notice she clutches a mug of coffee like a life preserver. It reads *Coffee first then adulting.* "Hello," she says, raking me up and down. "You're Leela's sister, right?"

"Mira." I nod and smile, pushing past her into the house uninvited.

"Right." She closes the door and turns to face me. "I have to get Sophie to school soon, so now isn't the best time."

"I will take her for you if you like." I perch on the arm of the over-stuffed sofa closest to the overly grand foyer. I wonder who dusts the chandelier.

"Not necessary, thanks. Why are you here?" she asks more pointedly, taking a step toward me and cupping her precious caffeine in both hands. I notice the dark crescents cut beneath her eyes and purse my lips.

"Are you feeling well?"

She seems taken aback but takes stock of her appearance and manner. "I'm fine. Just under a lot of stress since Peter left. Well, longer than that. I suppose since we had kids." She laughs it off.

"All of them?" I press.

She sucks in her cheeks as she ponders my question. "The third was the hardest. Tough pregnancy. Took a lot out of me. But I was a bit older when I had Sophie. I guess I never fully recovered my energy, but I wouldn't trade her for the world."

When Elle finishes speaking, her mouth drops open in surprise. She hadn't meant to divulge all that to me, but she couldn't really help it since I used magic when I asked the question.

"Of course," I say with a sympathetic smile. "I was actually wondering about that time in your life. Do you recall anything strange about Sophie's birth, for example?" I cross my legs and lean forward.

"It was difficult like the rest of the pregnancy. I nearly passed out. But then she made it through, and I heard her little cry. They plopped her on my chest, and I'll never forget. I swear I saw a rainbow around her for a split second. They said it was the lights being diffused through the stuff from my uterus they hadn't completely cleaned off, but I like to believe it was a sign."

Elle looks positively terrified now, and the cup in her hands quakes dangerously.

"Don't worry," I say, and she calms. "Was there any time when she might have been...switched? For another baby?"

"No. Not possible. She was with me twenty-four seven."

I conjure myself a cup of tea and send her mug over to the end table since she's in a trance. "And Achan? I mean Peter? Was he particularly interested in this child?"

"He wanted another boy. He was disappointed and didn't come around the hospital much after he first met her. He said something about green eyes. But her eyes are blue like mine. That's funny though when I think of it, considering how green all your siblings' eyes are."

I nod, sipping at my drink. It was no surprise Achan preferred a male body to take over. But green eyes? He'd been hoping for—or expecting—a Djinni. He wanted to take over a Djinn body and never have to worry about needing more power or switching bodies again. Thankfully, he hadn't realized whatever he'd done had worked at least to some extent. But what had he done? How had he gotten Djinn DNA into that child?

I stand and grasp Elle's shoulders gently but firmly. "What was it that was so hard with Sophie's pregnancy?"

"I was on and off bed rest through the whole thing. It's all so fuzzy, like I don't remember. I think I repressed the painful memories. I was so worried." A tear slides down her cheek, and the hatred I bear toward that man burns to my core.

I know where I must go next.

Stepping back, I send her mug into her hands, heating it up a bit for her. Then I release her and the memory of our conversation. "Thank you for your hospitality. I know you have to get Sophie to school."

Outside the house, I disappear once again. I never thought I'd return to that horrid place, but by now I should know to never say never.

With a wave of my arm, I fly over land and ocean, from beaches and crystal waters to rolling black waves with white foam caps that bubble like acid beneath me. The island is no longer there—I made sure it sank beneath the unforgiving tides—but I know the spot. I feel the dark magic in my veins, churning up memories like the waters below.

I dive below the surface and straight down into the depths of the freezing waters. I do not need to breathe like a human. I do not need the comfort of warmth, though I prefer both. I pass creatures that live like I did, on instinct and necessity, never thinking past the next moment.

The fortress comes into view, already covered in growing moss and other living matter clinging to its surface for purchase. I enter through the open top that used to tease us with the distant stars and down to the throne room where I swim forward until I reach the three statues, seated on their thrones. I head straight for Achan and float down to stand before him, my hair spread around me like a dark and twisted halo. I place a protective air bubble around us and dry myself quickly before doing what I must.

The stone cracks down the center, crumbling around him in piles, and he gasps for air as he comes to life once again. Beneath the stone, he is immortal. We were forced to make it so, but he has spent his days in madness. I hope.

"Mira?" He wheezes, taking stock of his current position. I suppose I can appreciate the classic features that first drew Leela to him. But to me, he is as ugly a man as I've ever seen because I know his soul. I think briefly of Rook and how he sees me, and warmth floods my chest.

"I have questions," I say, folding my arms before me.

"Of course. Anything." He stands, and my eyes glow until he sits again.

"You will answer me truthfully and clearly." I command it, and his anxious face goes slack. "What did you do during Sophie's pregnancy? To your wife?"

"Nothing to her. She was the vessel." His words are flat, but I shudder with disgust. Vessel?

"What did you do to the fetus?" I rephrase the question in a way his monstrous brain will understand.

"I was tired of switching bodies, and Jered was kept away from me. I used magic to impregnate Elle again and couldn't leave things to chance. I needed another option, and if the experiment worked, a Djinn body to keep forever."

"How? What was the experiment?" I lean over him, face-to-face, barely able to keep myself from scratching his eyes out.

"I bought Djinn blood. The man who sold it to me swore it was real. He was a magician and took it from his Djinni to sell and make more magicians. I injected it directly into the fetus through Elle's stomach using magic to pinpoint the safest location. I shouldn't have done it."

I straighten. Was this remorse? Is it possible? "Why not?"

"I lost a fortune on it, and it wasn't worth it. Sophie is a girl and not Djinn. Though I suppose I at least had a backup body."

I press my eyes closed and take a deep breath, forcing myself forward.

"Who was the man you bought from? What did he look like?" *Please don't let it be Rook.*

"You're shaking," Achan observes, and I snap my eyes open, stepping back.

"Did I not make my question clear enough?" Electricity sizzles at my fingertips, and I point at him.

"All I know is his code name was Raven. He couldn't have been more than a teenager. Lucky bastard had a Djinni. I tried to follow him once and take it by force, but he managed to disappear on me."

The electricity dies, and a whimper escapes my throat. *No.* I start to hyperventilate as I picture it. There was no Djinn slave, only Rook trying to fix everything with his blood. If he made this kind of horrible mistake, then who's to say there aren't a hundred—even a thousand Achans out there experimenting in horrible ways. The implications bring tears to my eyes because it is clear what must be done, and it may mean losing Rook.

15

IN THE BEGINNING

*W*HEN *R*HADA RETURNS A FEW DAYS LATER, *I* AM SITTING CROSS-LEGGED IN *the middle of the bed, indulging in a pomegranate, which I've opened with magic. The sticky red juice trickles down my face as I continue to coax the precious seeds from inside.*

Rhada's boisterous laugh echoes through the small house. "I see I've missed too much."

She bounces onto the bed to face me, and I pull the last half of the fruit toward me protectively.

"Not willing to share?" She pouts.

"When I find something I enjoy this much, I am keeping it," I tell her, along with a meaningful look. I lick the juice from my chin.

"I wish my body were covered in that juice," she says, leaning in and expecting a kiss.

I take another handful of seeds and pulp and stuff it in my mouth instead.

"Where were you?" I ask through the mouthful.

"I traveled to the Orient. I brought you a gift." Her eyes sparkle, and I glance at the small chest I bought at the market for my own collection. Her gift is inside, but we shall see when I fancy giving it to her.

I wait, magicking away the mess and licking my fingers clean as she unpacks a flowing silk robe from the air before her. It is thin and delicate with deep-blue, almost purple ink, dyed into white. She holds it up before me, and I see a scene with homes and bridges, waterfalls and fowl all around it.

Reaching forward after making certain my hands are clean, I let the magical fabric glide through my fingers like a whisper. My eyes grow wide. It is beautiful.

"It's like nothing I've ever seen." I leap from the bed and dance around, holding the outfit to my chest and twirling so that it swirls around me in a cloud of finely woven silk.

"Put it on!" Rhada claps with glee.

I slip off my current clothing and put the robe on, relishing the cool, smooth sensation where it touches my flesh. I hug myself.

"Thank you."

Rhada stands, opening her arms. "Am I forgiven then?"

I pretend to hesitate and then embrace her, opening my mouth in invitation. Perhaps she will receive some sweet remnant of the taste of the pomegranate.

The following day, I have the treasure behind my back as she sleeps. I watch her, so peaceful in slumber as I tuck a stray curl behind her ear. Like this, she feels delicate like the robe she gave me. When she's awake, her boisterous energy hides what appears now as a fragile nature. It is this secret Rhada that I love so dearly.

Her eyes flutter open, and I am greeted with a heart-stopping smile.

"Good morning," she says with a yawn as she sits, stretching in the morning sunlight spilling through the window.

"I have something for you." I hold out the small bundle.

She giggles and takes it, tugging at the outer wrappings.

"When you wear it, you will know that I am always with you and that it is my love that brings you home."

When Rhada reaches the final prize, her face lights with happiness, and my heart swells. She holds up the sparkling ruby that I've hung on a piece of velvet ribbon, and it twirls in the space between us, sending a galaxy of red stars all around the room.

"Oh, Mira! It's beautiful. You spoil me." She throws herself into my arms, knocking me back to the bed where we both laugh, giddy. She puts it around her throat and admires it, rolling it between her fingers, and then attacks me again with a passionate kiss.

She stays home for an entire month after I give her the necklace, and I know I've done well.

That morning I find Leela in the market, ducked behind the jeweler's cart. I laugh when I see her hiding.

"What are you doing?" I adjust the basket on my arm, and she yanks me down beside her, pointing toward a small group of people gathered around another vendor.

"Shh. Why is he talking to her again?" She hisses the question at me, and I squint, finding the only male in line of sight. That must be her human she's taken such a liking to. I see he is speaking to Kitra, who bats her eyes and adjusts her hair and outfit in a suggestive manner. I nearly laugh. Until I see Rhada is part of the group, that is.

She glares daggers at Lee's shepherd boy, and something sharp spears my heart. Is she jealous of Kitra's flirtations? When Kitra turns to include her, her face melts into a lovely smile. I use my nonhuman ears to listen to the conversation.

"Achan, this is my friend, Rhada."

The shepherd's smile falters, but only for a moment. "It is an honor. I have a friend with similar eyes. Quite beautiful."

Kitra's gaze bounces between them, something flashing behind it.

Beside me, Leela makes a small hmmph sound. "If he likes my eyes so much, why spend time looking in her dull ones?"

Having had enough, I shake my head and leave the drama to Leela and her suspicions. I have food to gather for dinner.

I should not have bothered. Rhada does not show up until far past time for food. The meal and my efforts are wasted. And when she does materialize, I immediately notice the missing gem from around her neck.

"Where have you been?" I all but bark at her, fists clenched at my sides.

She narrows her eyes, deciding whether or not to torture me by withholding the information. Apparently, my rage is enough to coax the truth from her.

"I was with Kitra." She slurs her words. I've never seen a Djinni drunk before and wonder if Kitra used some concoction on her. My anger boils into fear as the broken memories take hold.

"You should stay far away from that woman. She is sick."

"No, it is her father that is sick. But I helped her take care of that." She dances around in a circle, laughing.

"What does that mean?" I ask, the pitch of my voice uncomfortably high.

"I took a page from Taj's book. I killed the bastard. Don't look at me like that! Do you know what he'd done to her? Over and over again?" She gets in my face, and I recoil from the scent of her breath.

"Taj doesn't kill. He transforms," I say, weakly. I know what the man does —or did—to her. I also know what she did to me. If I told Rhada, would she kill her too? Or would she laugh at me and make some excuse?

Rhada's eyes flash. "He deserved what we did to him."

"What did you do?" I ask.

"I chained him to the wall, and we made him watch us make love." She laughs, delighted in herself. "Then I let her do the honors. I created a dagger for the occasion."

"She saw you do magic?" The thought of sharing our secret with humans sends my heart pounding. Especially this human.

Rhada shrugs. "She suspected, I think. She saw me react to the lead pots in the kitchens when we sneaked in to steal the spirits. She helped me away from them, Mira. She isn't bad."

My mouth becomes dry. "Where is the gift I gave you, Rhada?"

Her hand flutters to her neck as though she just now realizes it's gone.

"I left it there while we were making love. I'll get it back tomorrow when I see her again."

My vision blurs as my body tenses so much it shakes. "You cannot return tomorrow, Rhada."

"I can and I will. What's more, you should come too. You're invited. Whatever you may think of her, she seems to like you."

"Like she does Leela's shepherd?" I spit the words at her, but she only laughs again.

"He'll be there tomorrow as well as another man she told me about. I know it's because she plans to take over her father's position with them, but I think there'll be opportunity for fun also. She says the new guy has the biggest cock she's ever seen! Maybe the shepherd will bring Lee, and we can all have a party. Should I invite Taj?"

Rhada spins until she falls down across the bed, eyes closed. "The world is moving, Mira."

"If you go, I may not be here when you return." I rush from the house, tears burning the backs of my eyes as I run out of the village and through the desert to a rocky hill where all that remains is the sand scratching my throat and the moon and stars shining false promises above.

16

FINAL DESTRUCTION

Trembling with rage, I stare at the man before me. He is a man who has cheated death and cheated karma for far too long. Perhaps killing is wrong. Perhaps it is sometimes a mercy. But I am certain in this moment that sometimes it is a necessity that one must bear the repercussions for in order to free the conscience of others.

I can be that person. It's been forced from me so many times that though I value my autonomy above all else, I know that I'm more than capable of it. Perhaps this is my purpose, to carry out the actions that are too difficult for others.

"Shall I murder you?" I ask.

Still beneath my spell, Achan tilts his head at me and considers.

"I'd rather you didn't. Perhaps there's a way I can survive without endangering you."

I shake my head. "You will always be a danger to someone because no one's life means more to you than your own."

"Do you want to have my blood on your hands?" Achan asks, and I note the trickle of sweat beading on his brow despite my calming magic.

"Perhaps it is not about what I want any longer."

I release him from my spell, and he falls to his knees, tears springing from his eyes. He is pathetic. So why am I hesitating? How is this worse than putting him in stone?

"Do you have any final words?" I ask as he calms slightly.

"I won't accept that it ends like this." Achan stares up at me, his dark eyes filled with hate like boiling oil.

I know what he plans, and I'm faster, but at least this way I have little choice in the matter. I hesitate long enough for him to rise and pull the lead sword from the air above him. Then time slows, and from his feet to the tip of the sword, Achan becomes solid ice. He is frozen in an expression of fury, about to strike with his weapon, tip pointed down at me.

I reach forward and flick his arm. A crack starts at the point of contact and spreads up then outward around this ice sculpture until it is covered in veinlike fissures.

"Good-bye. I do not believe even an immortal can come back from this."

I place my fingertips to my lips and blow as though I'm sending him a kiss. Achan shatters into a billion sparkling particles of snow, scattering across the floor of the bubble I've made for us.

I stand still, staring at the tiny shards scattered on the ground at my feet. My breath flows heavy through my nose.

"You're next, Cephas," I say, turning to the giant in his throne. The bubble moves with me, encompassing both him and Kitra, still encased in stone. But I have something more in mind for my old master. One last conversation.

I flick my wrist, and Kitra's statue cracks and crumbles just as Achans did. When she stands, I immediately freeze her in place so all she can do is speak. I do not trust her, and I will not make a mistake by letting my guard down.

"What is this?" she demands.

"You think you are still a queen?" I ask, circling her. "You never were. You missed me saying good-bye to Achan. I thought you may want to watch with Cephas."

I reach around from behind her and snap in front of her face. Cephas too comes back to life with a mighty roar, standing and seething as his beady eyes find and focus on me behind Kitra.

"Enough! I have been frozen as a statue for far too long," he bellows.

I step out from behind Kitra, and he and I circle each other at a distance of a few feet. Oh, how we all used to fear his enormous stature and bestial tendencies. But they were all the same in the end, selfish and sadistic.

"You are going to die now, no more stone," I promise him, focused only on my own rage.

He laughs. "Let's fight hand to hand. That's the only fair fight for one of you."

I grin. "When have you ever been fair in your dealings?"

He lunges for me, and I decide just this once to hit him where it hurts. I spin, sending an uppercut right below his jaw. Cephas flies backward, landing on the ground. He yowls in pain, and I wait as he stands again, mouth askew from the dislocated joint. Now there is murder in his eyes. When he speaks, it's hard to understand, but I figure it out.

"I will cover you in lead and teach you what you're good for." He cracks his knuckles, and thick lead rings appear on his meaty fingers. "Leela liked this."

I freeze him there and then. No need to play with him further. I repeat the same motions I took with Achan, flicking him to start the cracking and then blowing him apart to scatter on the ground.

"Your turn." I spin toward the woman who started all of this. The one who killed Rhada, enslaved Leela, and then the rest of us. The mastermind behind a thousand years of torture and pain for more people than I can count. Possibly the most dangerous woman in the world.

"You have different plans for me. I can tell," she says, still frozen as I step so close, I can feel her hot breath.

"Because you know everything." I cup her face in my hand. "Was this what it felt like, Kitra? When you had complete power over me and could do anything you fancied just to see how I would react?"

Her eyes widen as much as she is able. "What are you going to do?"

I stroke her lips with my thumb and shush her. "I'll tell you what I'm not going to do. I'm not going to drug you with a so-called spell."

I pull my finger away as she snaps at it, trying to bite me. "Now is that the way to treat the one with all the power? I thought you taught me differently."

"Go ahead and kill me then if that's what you're after. I'll never break. Not the way you want me to."

I smack her hard across the face. "I don't expect you to break emotionally. I could do it, though, Kitra. I could freeze you bit by bit and shatter each part of you until you beg me to end it."

She snaps her mouth shut, but I see the flare in her nostrils, the hate sparking in her eyes.

"I bet the idea of it turns you on, doesn't it? If our positions were reversed."

"I remember that day, Mira. I remember when you stole that ruby. You wanted it so bad I gave it back to you until you destroyed it. But as I recall, you enjoyed everything I did the night before. You may not like it, but I know what drives you."

I grab her wrist, and ice spreads out from there up to her shoulder. When I release her, both her arms and legs are frozen solid.

"You don't want to admit it, but it's easier for you when you have no choice, no control. You enjoyed being mine." Her shivering voice grates against my ears. There is so much wrath that it is hard to find the will to speak.

"You wish that were true, perhaps. Maybe that's how you were able to sleep at night. But I loathed every moment, every touch, and every word."

"I'll find a way back."

"There is no way back from this." My eyes glow, bathing her body in green as the rest of her finishes turning to ice, starting with her poisoned tongue.

I flick her forehead, sending cracks down over her body, and then I touch my lips once again, staring into her clear eyes as I blow across her face.

Her head goes first, disintegrating into such fine particles that it may as well be dust. Then the rest of her follows. When I'm done, I shrink the bubble to fit just my body and watch the waters of the Atlantic carry away any hope of our former masters returning from the dead.

17

TRUTH HURTS

I TRY TO SLEEP, MOSTLY SO I CAN AVOID THE NEXT DAY OR SO, BUT IT doesn't come easy. I dream of Rhada and the anger that fueled me the night I last saw her, and then the scenery changes as is often the nature of dreams. I find myself in a field with Rook standing on the opposite side. He holds out his arms to me, and I start to run, but I cannot reach him. Then another path presents itself, one that leads through the desert to Rhada where she is chained to Kitra's wall and the monster holds a lead knife to her neck. I can save her, but I will lose the path to Rook.

In the dream, I drop to my knees, unwilling to flee toward either goal. That is when Leela steps in front of me and pulls a tasseled cord, dropping a bloodred curtain in my way. She begins to laugh as I claw at the velvet, unable to move it.

"Tick tock," she says.

I wake, gasping and sweating in my bed, blankets twisted and sheets pulled free. I rush to the bathroom and cup water in my hands to splash on my face. The curtains are closed tight, but the clock reads three p.m. I'm not even sure what day it is anymore.

Destroying the Council was not as satisfying as I'd hoped, but how can I expect an hour to make up for a thousand years?

I pull on a soft white robe and brew some tea to curl up in my favorite armchair. I snap, and soft classical music surrounds me. The sound almost immediately irks me, and I snap again, blasting modern metal instead. No one will hear it outside my apartment.

I nearly spit out my mouthful of peppermint tea when Rook pops in a foot away. I stand, and the music stops.

"You didn't have to do that on my account. I like Metallica." He grins, and it's super sexy, which doesn't help.

I knew I'd have to face him, but I thought I'd have a bit more time to gather my thoughts.

"We need to talk." Misery drips from my voice.

He raises an eyebrow. "That's never good."

I take his hand, and he sits on my chair so I can climb in his lap. His smell is so comforting, and I can't help but lean into his chest. He raises his hand to my head, stroking my hair like it's automatic.

"This is about the other hybrid I know." I'm not sure how to start this conversation, but this seems as good a place as any.

He smiles. "That's certainly not the worst thing you could have said."

"I'm not done yet," I warn, taking a fistful of his shirt. "See, she's a hybrid *not* by love."

Rook shifts beneath me, tilting my chin up to face him. "You mean a Djinni slave was impregnated by a master? That's horrible."

"No. That's not what happened. I'm afraid it was worse, if that's possible." I sigh, trying to streamline my thoughts as he waits far too patiently. "The magician in question, the father, he stayed alive for centuries by taking possession of his own magical children's bodies. He wanted to find a way to ensure he could use the same body and never die. So he took Djinn blood and injected it, repeatedly, directly into the fetus through his pregnant wife's belly. His human wife."

I wait as Rook digests the information. The only movement I see is his Adam's apple bobbing slightly in his throat. When he says nothing, I continue.

"It was your blood, Rook." I say the words clearly but softly, embracing him as though I can prevent him from falling apart.

"Impossible," he says, standing so that I'm forced to as well. "What makes you think it was mine?"

"He said the code name of the man who sold it to him was Raven. It was a bit over a decade ago. You had probably just started. I knew it was you when he said he tried to follow you to take your Djinni, but you disappeared on him."

Rook's body turns to jelly, and he falls back into the chair. I wait for it to sink in, unsure what to expect, or hope for.

"A decade, you say? What is his name?"

"His real name was Achan, but he went by Peter back then, if he even told you that much truth." I put a slight emphasis on the past tense in my reply. He is no longer available to speak to, if that's what Rook is thinking.

Rook nods. "I remember him. He was one of the first. I saw the lies in his aura, the way his energy shifted tight around his throat."

"If you saw it, then why did you allow it?" Unbelievable. I fold my arms before me and jut out my hip.

He clutches the arms of the chair and peers up at me.

"I was young and told myself he was afraid."

"He *was* afraid."

"Let me finish. Afraid of losing the love of his life. That was his story. He said he loved a human woman so much that he couldn't bear to be without her and that once she'd found out about his abilities, she fell into a deep depression because she could never truly share his life. A beautiful story."

I cock my head in disbelief. "Story is the key word here. He made it up to manipulate you, and you fell for it. Do you know the pain his actual human wife must have endured? He adjusted her memories so many times, there were side effects according to Leela and Taj. Not to mention the danger Sophie, his own child, was put into."

He stands to meet me and puts out his hands as if to embrace me, and I take a step back. "Mira, I take responsibility. I was wrong, and it was a mistake. Is that what you want to hear?"

"Partially," I confess, unfolding my arms. "But it's more than that, Rook, and you know it."

He runs a hand through his hair and paces. "You used names. Sophie? That's the child's name? And Leela and Taj...you know this hybrid? This magician you speak of? Wait." He comes to a sudden stop before me, face paling. "You already knew something about this."

"I don't know what that has to do with anything. I had to make sure I was right. I had to know how she came to be before I told you."

"Mira." He says my name while running his hands down over his face. "We need to trust each other and be open from the very start if this is going to work. When something big like this comes up, I want you to feel like you can tell me so we can face it together."

I shake my head as though clearing it as I try to process what he's saying. I have too many questions.

"If what is going to work?" I start with that one.

"Us. Our relationship." He smiles and holds out his hands to me again.

"You are distracting me from the issue," I accuse. "How many of these mistakes have you made while being so naïve?" I stride past him and sit on the chair, legs crossed.

"I believe in humanity, Mira. That's not to say there aren't terrible people, but the vast majority—"

"You are blind," I shout and at once regret the words, his literal disability forgotten.

Rook's head snaps back as though I've physically slapped him. He stumbles backward a few feet and rubs at his face again.

"I'm so sorry," I say, standing and reaching out. "I didn't mean—" But I can't finish the sentence because what did I mean? His refusal to see truth makes the existence of his black market dangerous.

I take a few cleansing breaths, my chest growing steadily heavier with the weight of inevitability. "I can't let you continue to sell DB. It is far too dangerous."

"I hate to inform you of this, but it's not your decision." The sharp pain between his words stabs me as he speaks.

"Unfortunately for you, I represent the Order, and I have the power to shut down the black market."

Golden sparks fly from his amber eyes, and my mouth drops open.

"I didn't say you couldn't. I said it's not your place, Mira. I don't answer to the Order. You need to decide who you are. Are you a monster like those who enslaved you, forcing your will upon others? Thinking that you know best? Or are you my equal, who can discuss, disagree, and even persuade, but never change me? Please think before you answer because I can't be with the former."

My throat dries up, and tears burn at the backs of my own glowing eyes. I don't know what I expected to happen, but the problem is that what I need to do and what I want to do are two very different things. I recall how it felt to blast each of my former masters into stardust and stare at my hands. Did I have the right to decree judgment? It was personal, but shouldn't I have asked Lee and Taj before I did so?

Rook takes my silence as something else. Or maybe he's heard my thoughts, and what I've done disgusts him.

"I'll give you some time to think. You know where I'll be. Just remember Daffodil and her grandson. Or do you think he's made up now too?"

He doesn't give me a chance to answer, not that I'm sure I could. He disappears from the room, and I'm left with a deafening silence and such a heavy heart that I collapse onto my knees as the tears finally break through.

18

TEA WITH GRANDMAMAN

I SETTLE MY NERVES THE WAY I ALWAYS DO, BY THROWING MYSELF INTO MY work. Two unassigned Djinn remain on my list to be freed, so I send one to Taj and Cal, and take the last for myself. I'd give it to Leela, but I'm worried about her illness. It's best not to put her at risk if possible until we know more.

The case I choose is the one closest to France. May as well stop by on my way to the Vatican. Naturally, overly trusting Rook has left access to his magic server on my phone, which I use to follow Daffodil's trail to her home outside Paris. The elderly woman lives in a fairy tale from what I can tell. The villa is a picturesque enlargement of a cottage, surrounded by rolling hills, vineyards, and brightly colored gardens. The thatched roof and stark painted trim give the whole thing the feel of an idyllic landscape painting. The scent of fresh baked fruit pie and roses fills my senses as I approach the double doors with a brass knocker.

I stay invisible as I float inside. No need to alarm her as long as she's telling the truth. I find her seated in a hand-carved rocking chair with a pile of knitting in her lap, the shiny needles dancing in the air before her as she reads a novel, spectacles balanced at the tip of her nose.

I am about to peek at the book when footsteps tumble down the stairs. A tall and gangly young man with a bright-white aura bounces into the room with long dark hair that falls in his face and startlingly blue eyes that practically light up against his mahogany skin. Daffodil's entire being also lights up as she lifts her face to greet him.

"How are you feeling, Devon dear?"

"Like a million dollars, Grandmaman. And look what I can do!"

Devon pops into nothingness and reappears on the opposite side of his grandmother's chair with a laugh. I find myself smiling along with them until his head snaps up like a dog who's scented something on the wind, and he narrows his eyes in my direction.

"I can feel you. Show yourself." He steps protectively in front of his grandmother.

I could run. Pretend I was never here. But I'm curious, and my decision is made swiftly as I appear before them.

"Hello, Devon. Daffodil." I nod at the grandmother peering around the side of her still-growing grandson. "I didn't mean to alarm you, and I apologize for the intrusion."

"Who are you?" Devon demands.

I'm only slightly surprised to see his blue eyes glow unnaturally brighter. Apparently, hybrid blood creates hybrids and not magicians, or it has something to do with his age and development.

"It's okay, Devon. This is a friend of mine. She helped get the Djinn blood for you. For all we know, it may be her own blood that's helping you heal."

Devon relaxes a bit but shoots me an I-still-don't-trust-you look, which makes me admire him all the more.

"It isn't mine, but I would have been glad to help," I say.

Daffodil scoots Devon's lanky form out of the way and stands far more spryly than I would have guessed possible.

"Why don't we all have some tea? I have a fresh peach-and-blueberry pie in the kitchen."

"That sounds divine." I follow her and Devon through a hall filled with family pictures and into a large eat-in kitchen where I sit at the shining wooden table, light streaming in through the window and onto the surface.

"Would it be rude to ask your real name?" Daffodil says as a cup and saucer float my way along with sugar cubes and milk.

"That's rude?" Devon grumbles as he sits on the opposite side of me. "Not her barging in our house and spying?"

"Devon!" Daffodil snaps, and he sits up straight.

"The boy isn't wrong," I say, tipping some piping hot liquid into my cup and inhaling the aroma of cinnamon and chamomile. "Mira *is* my real name."

"Mine is Alice." She joins us at the table and sends the teapot floating into her hand so she can serve herself.

I take a sip of the divine brew as pie is served by invisible hands all around. Devon immediately digs in.

"I can't stay long," I warn, cupping the warmth in my hands. "But this is lovely."

"Do tell us why you came," Alice says, stirring in some milk and sugar.

I clear my throat and shift uneasily in the seat. "I had to make sure you meant what you said. That you told us the truth the other night."

Alice nods, smiling, and takes a sip. "And?"

"Everything appears to be in order." I nod at Devon.

"My grandmaman doesn't lie." Devon stabs a forkful of pie and chews as he glares my way.

"You never know," I say, gesturing with my fork. "People do lie more often than you think. In the wrong hands, Djinn blood can be a dangerous commodity."

"I can only imagine the things you've seen," Alice says with a sigh. "My grandpapa had a Djinni in his possession. I sneaked in and freed him as a rebellious teenager. When he found out, he gave me this scar with the beating I got." She holds up her arm and pulls up her sleeve to reveal an aged welt the size and shape of a whiplash. "I'd do it again in a heartbeat."

I raise an eyebrow. "I can fix that for you if you'd like."

"No, thank you, dear." She pulls her sleeve down and picks up her tea. "It's a bit of a badge of honor to me."

Warmth and admiration fill my heart, and I sit back with relief, knowing I hadn't misjudged her. The pie tastes extra delicious now.

"So where is your young man if you don't mind my asking?" Alice says, staring with interest at her plate.

I sigh heavily in response, and she sets down her own fork to focus on me. "What happened?"

"I found out that someone he gave the blood to did a very bad thing," I admit, pushing away my food.

"That's why you came to check on us?" Devon asks.

Alice shushes him, but I wave it off.

"He's right." I tell them the situation without names and without gory details, though I'm sure Alice understands the blood was delivered unwillingly at the very least as her shrewd old eyes crinkle.

We all sit silent for a minute. Then Devon is the one to speak.

"That's messed up."

"Agreed," I say.

"So you're wondering if it's all worth it." Alice places an unexpectedly soft hand over mine. "What that man did was horrible. But it wasn't Raven's fault, nor was it yours. That's on him and his soul. Have you met the child?"

I glance over at her. "Yes. I know her. She's got a heart of gold. In fact, she saved my brother from being a slave. Maybe all of us."

"How old did you say she is?" Devon's jaw drops open.

"She was eight at the time." I grimace with the memory of being forced to stand guard over her. I hated the fear flowing off her tiny body.

"Then it sounds like this is perhaps an example of something good coming from something evil." Alice pats my hand and then her mouth with a napkin. "I know you are probably older than I am by quite a bit, Mira. But if you don't mind me sharing my experience with you, I've learned that when something good is meant to happen, it finds a way. Even in the darkest hour, the light is ready to break through, but sometimes we have to give a little assist if we can."

"Like you reaching out to Raven for help with Devon," I say.

She nods.

I push away from the table and wave an arm, cleaning the mess. "Thank you for the lovely visit, Alice. Next time I promise to knock."

"Do you have to go so soon? I'd like to know more about Djinn and what I can do now."

I swing around to face Devon, shocked that he wants me to stay, yet pleased.

"I'll have to come again soon, then. But right now, I have a Djinni to free."

19

IN THE BEGINNING

ANOTHER WEEK GOES BY WITHOUT A WORD FROM RHADA. I TRY TO CHECK IN with the others and receive only the same old message from Leela. That I shouldn't worry so. That she's probably just playing with her human. Well, how would she feel if her shepherd were to play with another human? Kitra even? I saw how he looked at her in the market and how worried Leela was. She was being such a hypocrite that it angered me to the point I had to leave. This is a problem I'll have to deal with on my own.

But as time marches on, I find I am not dealing with it well at all. I don't leave the house anymore for fear she will turn up and I'll miss her. How could I let her go like that with so much anger? Surely she knows that I want her back.

She left before I returned that night. No note. No message other than the one clearly stated by her absence. In my heart, I know she's gone back to Kitra, but I fear what I'd see if I went in search of her. I fear even more what I'd do in order to keep her in my life.

I thought she'd return after the debilitating pain we all experienced. When it tore through my heart like a million knives carving me open, I fell to the ground and screamed her name. Crying and repeating it again and again long after the pain passed. I ran to Taj, and then Leela came again. We all felt it. All came back.

All except Rhada.

"Why can't you be happy with just me?" I scream at the top of my lungs. I scream until my throat is raw and my voice is rasped. But still nothing answers save the whisper of the wind outside my window.

It is at this point, seated on my knees in the middle of a house that does not even feel like my own, that I wonder why I am here in this body if not for Rhada. I need the touch of another while I can experience it. So I run to Taj and find him alone, much to my relief. But that relief lasts only a moment when I see the worried expression on his handsome face.

"Taj?" I am tentative as I reach for him.

He pulls me into a firm embrace and speaks into my hair. "Oh, thank the gods, Mir. I thought you all disappeared on me."

"What happened?" I ask, pulling away to see his face.

"I haven't seen Lee in a very long time. And I haven't seen you even longer. And Rhada? I don't even know when the last time she checked in was."

I swallow hard, looking away. "I'm starting to think this place may not be as heavenly as we first thought."

We sit together, and that helps despite the silence. I'm not sure how much time passes before I feel the rustle of leaves around us in the olive branches. When I look, Leela stands before us. But her face is gaunt, her eyes filled with sorrow and confusion.

Taj stands, greeting her, asking where she's been. She doesn't say much, only begs us to follow her. I'm tired of following others and doing as they please. I want a chance to decide my own path. The only trouble is without Rhada, I'm not sure what that is.

And then she says her name, and everything changes.

"It's Rhada. She's in trouble. Please, you have to come."

Leela disappears, and I jump to my feet. Of course I'll follow. If Rhada is in trouble, then that is why she has not returned. It isn't that she chose someone else. My heart leaps into my throat as Taj and I take each other's hands and appear after Lee at a familiar home that freezes my heart.

Naturally she's with Kitra. She's probably spelled her like she did me. I rush through the door, Taj at my heels, and am ambushed by the weight and pain of lead chains thrown around my throat. The lead sears into my flesh, and I drop to my knees, barely aware of Taj suffering beside me. We're pulled into another room, one that I've never been in, and I find the chains snaking around my entire body, binding my arms and legs together like a mummy. The metal burns my clothing, and each bit of flesh it touches is a brand-new agony.

But as time passes and the pain only increases, my voice silences because I no longer have the strength to cry out. That is when I look around me for the first time to find Taj in the same situation and...

My heart stops beating. I swear it does. Rhada is here, but something is very wrong. She's chained to the wall, but does not look like herself. Her body is swollen and stiff, her eyes bulging and lifeless. Her skin almost blue and so tight around her bones that I'm surprised I recognize her.

She is devoid of life.

"Rhada," I whisper, and Taj glances up, tears spilling from his eyes. "Nooooo." It is a cry of misery from my very soul, deeper than the pain of any lead. It isn't possible. It shouldn't be possible.

After another indeterminable amount of time, I notice the remains of Kitra's father chained beside Rhada just as she had described to me. Then it occurs to me that Leela is not here with us. Has she escaped? Will she free us? She must have discovered Rhada's body and panicked. If only she'd warned us so we could prepare.

As if in answer to my question, Lee enters the room, unaffected by the presence of the lead. I spot Kitra behind her, her bright-red-and-black aura flowing over Leela. Protecting her? But Leela is paler than I've ever seen. Something in her eyes is not right. They look...clouded as she kneels before Taj.

That is when I see her take a ribbon from Kitra's hand. On the center sits a glowing tiger's eye pendant. I've seen that stone before. Now that I search for it, I find the opal from Kitra's collection around Leela's neck, bound tight like a choker. Leela places the tiger's eye pendant around Taj's neck, and his chains fall off; the largest man I've ever seen stands above him. Taj kneels beside him, shoulders shaking as he cries.

When Leela turns toward me, I can't watch, so I look to Rhada's blank face. I notice she does not wear the ruby I gave her. I assume it's back in Kitra's collection. Leela is saying something. I turn to see her holding up the ruby, and I begin to understand. These are collars, not jewelry. They mark us as Kitra's slaves. The choker tightens against the pulse of my throat.

"Why?" I ask, still trying to process everything. If she had the opal on when she retrieved us, and I realize now she did, then she knew what was happening.

Kitra's essence falls away before Leela's mouth fully opens, and the Djinni drops to the floor, writhing in pain. I watch, detached as Kitra leans down over me and whispers.

"You will soon see she had no choice. None of you do anymore."

Kitra sends Leela flying out of the room like a sack of rice. The giant man drags Taj out, and the door slams shut as Kitra towers above me.

I'm faintly aware of the lead chains lying around me in a pile. Of barely holding my naked body up with my hands pressed to the ground.

Kitra cups my face, and I try to pull away but am too weak.

"You thought you could steal from me, Mira? And I trusted you."

"You can't be trusted," I rasp the words out, each one a dagger dragging along my throat.

She squeezes my face now, the tips of her crimson nails digging into my flesh.

"You and your lover, Leela, this new male, all you ever wanted was to manipulate humans like we were the toys, keep the magic out of our grasp and all for yourselves. Now the tables have turned. We are the ones worthy of the power. You wanted this ruby so badly?" She releases my face to touch the jewel at the base of my neck. "You thought I wouldn't recognize it around Rhada's throat?"

I don't answer. She'll only twist my reply. But this cannot be about a jewel. If it is, I'll offer her a thousand.

"She gave it to me willingly, you know. I believe it was while she begged for her life. It's a shame we didn't know then that there is a limit on the power we can take on by consuming your kind's blood. I'd love to have her as a slave as well. But you will do."

"I will never comply, murderer." I hiss the words at her.

She answers with a smile that makes my blood run cold. "Consider this ruby a gift. I have another after all. Its twin keeps you under my control. You will obey my every command, Mira. And you will refer to me as 'Master.'"

I stare at her in defiance, my vision beginning to blur around the edges.

"Call me Master."

The word leaps from my mouth without my consent. "Master."

"Good. Now rise and follow me."

Despite the searing pain in my body, I somehow stumble to my feet and follow after her outside the room. The farther we leave the lead behind, the stronger my limbs become, but at no point do I stop following her, even as she parades me past the others, the giant's lecherous gaze raping my body from a distance even as Taj kneels before him.

I instantly cover myself in a dress, and Kitra spins on me as though she felt it, bringing me to a halt. Her dark eyes flash.

"Did I say you could do that?" Her spit flies in my face.

"No, but—"

The back of her hand swipes across my cheek, knocking me backward. Tears sting my eyes as I touch the spot.

"Take it off."

The dress vanishes as I swallow away any other protests.

"Good. Now tell me why you did that."

"I did not like how the men looked at me." I stand as straight as possible, relishing the fact that I am at least a bit taller than Kitra.

"You mean the other Council members?" Kitra gestures toward Cephas, who is now examining Taj like a sheep meant for market, and Leela's shepherd boy, who wears the fine silk robes of a king. Leela stands meekly behind him, refusing to meet my eyes.

"Yes, apparently that's who they are."

"You will address them with respect. Cephas. Achan. Please join us. You two go to your rooms." To my dismay, the men come closer, surrounding me while Leela leads Taj down the hall, leaving me utterly alone.

"It seems you've made my slave uncomfortable with your stares. Perhaps she will become used to your presence more easily if you each spend some quality time together."

My mouth drops open, and I begin to tremble as the men ogle the parts of my body I'd longed to cover. Does she mean for them to rape me? I think of the time she'd done things to me herself in her room. She'd probably like to watch.

But I don't have to obey them. Do I?

As the giant grabs for my arm, I lash out, and they are both blown backward across the room.

"You can make me obey you, Kitra, but I refuse to suffer this indignity for your pleasure." I turn toward her and immediately take a step back. I've never seen such hate on a human face.

Without a word, she pulls a whip from the air and lashes it out against the wall, the sudden, ear-splitting sound making me wince.

"It's lined with lead. And you will obey their commands as long as they mean me no harm. Is that understood?"

"Yes."

"You will refer to me as Master. You will never address me by my familiar name again."

"Yes, Master."

"Kneel."

I drop to one knee, head bowed in humiliation. She whips me, drawing screams from each lash against my flesh. Blood splatters across the great room and hall as she continues in a frenzy. I roll on the ground, trying to protect myself from a second hit over the long, deep gashes, but the sting and sizzle find every part of me, relentlessly.

I sense the others back on their feet, gathered round. When I can no longer move except for the jerk of my body at each lick of the whip, that is when she stops. I stare up at the blood-splattered face of the giant leaning over me. Slowly, his lips draw wide in a grin, revealing rotten teeth and a putrid smell that causes me to vomit.

"Get up, slave. And clean up the mess. Cephas, teach her some manners and give her to Achan when you're done with her."

I am already climbing to my feet and waving away the blood and gore even as I heal. Kitra is long gone by the time Cephas tosses me over his shoulder and carries me screaming off to his rooms.

20

TO FREE A DJINNI

THE MOMENT I STEP FOOT ON THE GROUNDS OF THE VATICAN, ALL MY senses sharpen, and my mind focuses solely on my mission. I cannot afford to lose a millisecond of attention to other stresses and worries. Perhaps that's why I love this job so very much.

That and I'm damn good at it.

I'm not invisible, but I mill inside with the other tourists, hiding my face with sunglasses and a visor so that I do not appear on anyone's radar. I conjured myself a tiny golden cross to wear on a delicate chain so that it sparkles at my clavicle. I don't like wearing necklaces, but I thought it a nice touch considering I'm posing as a good little Catholic girl.

The only information we have on this Djinni is that they are kept inside the vault, and only the highest-ranking officials—and even then, only select ones—have access. The owner is not the Pope, nor are we certain whether he is aware of the Djinni's existence or not. The master, from what we've gleaned, is an elderly bishop who has handpicked his successor and trained him.

The vault likely contains quite a bit that humans are unaware of, perhaps quite a bit we Djinn are ignorant of as well. Anticipation tingles down to my toes as I follow the throngs deep inside the maze of buildings. It's a heady mixture of excitement along with the promise of danger and the unknown.

When the crowd thins out a bit, to the rear of a building, I reach out with my senses and find the auras of several magicians spread around the entire complex. This could be trickier than I thought. I fan out farther, pretending to stare at my phone. Beneath my feet, magic pulses, ebbs, and swells, humming through me in a rhythm something like a heartbeat. I find two magicians there, tucked inside the catacombs several levels beneath the basement. I feel more than that, though, and I wonder if it is the Djinni's own magic or something else that calls to me. I shudder slightly and tap the screen in my hand, shooting off a quick message to Taj to let him know where I am and what is happening. It's a precaution I feel comfortable with since the events of the year previous, when being unsure of each other's situations caused far too much mayhem.

Satisfied, I square my shoulders, glance around for any cameras or onlookers, and go invisible before falling down through the floors below my feet until I land on the solid yet uneven rock at the bottom-most level.

I land in a crouch, eyes narrowed and focused so that I can take in my surroundings and any immediate danger. What I find are walls of shelves, inlaid into the natural rock and glowing with inset lights, holding artifacts and wealth beyond imagination. Figures and vases lined with gold and encrusted with jewels sit spaced in perfect increments as far as I can see. Some I immediately identify as belonging in certain eras and geographical locations belonging to history. Others are unfamiliar to me, and I eye them with suspicion and a certain level of awe.

Standing, I glance in both directions. I sense movement to my right, deeper into the darkened passage where lights flicker from what appear to be torches on the walls. For a moment, my chest squeezes, picturing the dungeons in Kitra's island fortress. But I shake that off and creep forward, trailing the movement.

Voices come into focus as I reach the curve of a natural pathway. I feel the lead's presence before I see its source. Enormous double doors crafted of iron and lined with the deadly substance are pulled open, offering passage into a rounded-out room of sorts, filled with glowing lights of various colors. Inside stand two men, backs to me. One is taller than the other, older too by the looks of his white hair peeking out from beneath his headdress. His robes sweep the ground. The man next to him is dressed slightly less ostentatiously, without a hat to cover his close-cropped dark hair. He clasps his perfectly manicured hands behind the small of his slender back.

I edge forward, being sure to stay far enough away from the lead in the doors to prevent being incapacitated or worse. But from this better vantage point, I can make out the sources of the glowing lights. I hold in my gasp.

Cages made of brightly colored glowing energy bars hold creatures of all manner. Each one is about five feet high, forcing some of the taller occupants to crouch, sit, or kneel. My gaze roves over the few in my line of sight, my brain struggling to find names for some of them. I spot what appears to be a fairy, with pointed ears and wings; a humanesque creature covered in matted brown fur, who fills almost its entire cage; and a...gremlin? Fury rises in me with the understanding that the Djinni is also within one of these cells. That all these creatures are being held against their will.

A sound from behind causes me to spin along with the magicians. I stare hard into the relative darkness, but nothing happens. It isn't enough for the men, though. The older one nods to the younger, and he darts past me into the catacombs. I'm forced to flatten against the wall so that he doesn't accidentally touch me as he passes.

I don't like it. They are now on high alert even though I was not the one to do it. Should I strike now? What if there's more lead inside? What if the Djinni isn't caged or is allowed to respond to defend their master?

Damn it.

The old bishop holds himself in profile, and the cold, calculated look on his face freezes me in place. His steel-gray eyes narrow, and his lip curls upward in distaste, forcing the many wrinkles on his skin to crumple into deep crags.

I've watched religions come and go, or stay and grow, over my many years, though admittedly from a distance. I've seen people twist and corrupt themselves and others, and I've seen yet more delude themselves while striving to find a reasonable explanation for the unexplainable.

This supernatural jail is the worst example of greed and power next to the master/slave dynamic. I will end it. But I must be smart about how.

They've kept this secret and who knows how many others for a very long time.

Awkward minutes later, the younger man returns, and the bishop relaxes his stance.

I find myself relaxing as well until the younger man speaks.

"You will release your Djinni now or face the consequences."

I recognize Leela's voice, and every muscle in my body clenches. What the hell is she doing?

"If you want the demon, come retrieve her yourself." The older man answers the question without a hint of surprise or dismay. If anything, I'd say he appears eager.

My gaze drops to his clenched hand sporting a large garnet ring in an ornate, tarnished setting. He calls her a demon yet finds no shame in controlling her. Hypocrite.

I feel the breeze of power coming down the hall and throw out a shield to prevent Leela from flying into the room or the lead trap that awaits. I grasp her in my arms, holding her struggling body against mine until she realizes it's me. Then I pull her back into the catacombs so we can chat.

"What the fuck are you doing?" I ask, sparks shooting from my eyes.

"I'm freeing the Djinni that you haven't gotten around to yet." Her chest puffs out in challenge, her eyes flash green as well.

"Obviously I'm here. You know I take my job seriously. You could have made this situation a million times worse by barging in there. They're expecting that, you know."

"I don't care." Leela crosses her arms and glares in the direction of the secret jail.

"Well, you should. The doors are lined with lead, and who knows what else is in there or what magic they wield."

Leela relaxes enough to look confused, and I sigh with relief. She hadn't even made it far enough in to see the situation.

"They have more than just a Djinni in there. There are others as well, and I'm betting they aren't too happy about being kept captive."

"All the more reason to save them," Leela says, voice softer now.

"Then let's do this together and think it through." I step back to lean against the wall.

"I'm waiting." The bishop's voice booms across the caverns, perhaps magically amplified. "Or are you afraid of being in the presence of one who walks with God?"

I roll my eyes.

Leela speaks, and her voice comes through faintly from behind me and through the other man's mouth.

"It is you who should fear the wrath of God, should she exist. Do you think God desires her creatures to be harmed or enslaved?"

I smile at her and squeeze her arm. "You transfer the doors upstairs, I will scan for more dangers, and then we enter together. You free the others, and I will remove the bishop's ring and see how smug he is then."

Leela grins wickedly, and we turn toward the path, taking each other's hands in silent support.

We rush forward, faster than humans can comprehend, and the heavy doors disappear from view. I reach inside with my senses and find no more obvious lead.

I appear before the bishop, and we drop hands. Leela remains invisible as I keep my glowing eyes trained on the man before me. He does not cower, but it is because of overconfidence in his own tricks. He will soon learn to believe otherwise.

"The devil tries, but Satan never wins." The man holds his chin up high, attempting to look down his nose at me.

I cock my head, knowing he will call his Djinni at any moment. But Leela has already taken care of that by restraining her in lead shackles.

Behind him, the electric bars of each colorful cage blink into nothingness.

"Give me the ring willingly." I hold out my hand.

He laughs and holds his hand up before me. "Kill this devil."

He barks the command at the air, and I raise my eyebrow, waiting for the full realization to hit him. Meanwhile, a half circle of creatures surround him from behind, rage seething into the air in a cloud of energy that makes me want to step away.

"I will take it then." I hold up a hand as if to say one moment and then grab his ring finger.

The old man is more skilled than I expect, and I am surprised to find myself thrown off-balance as his booted foot connects with my abdomen.

The breath is knocked from my lungs, but only for a moment as I rise again, eyes glowing with pleasure that this won't be quick. He clearly commanded the Djinni provide him with more personal abilities needed in order to procure these other beings, like superstrength and agility.

I find it odd that he's so focused on me, to the point of not seeming to notice his entire slew of captured beasts freed. They all stand back, as though they sense that I need this fight, Leela now standing among them.

"God is with me. You cannot harm me."

"If it's God with you, then why did you have to ask for this power from someone like me?" We circle each other, watching and waiting for our opponent to move.

"God works in mysterious ways," he says with a shrug.

I feint to the right and then lunge to the left, slowing time and grabbing his wrist to twist behind his back, my other arm secured around his neck. His aura flows out and over toward the wall, sending a set of vases and vials flying toward me. But I spin out of the way, pulling him with me. Black smoke explodes on the floor where they shatter, and a skull made of wispy gray curls into the air, laughing before dissipating.

I've never seen this type of magic before, and I don't want to see it again. I twist his wrist harder, hearing and feeling the bones crack and sinew tear as I wrench it away from his body.

The old man crumples before me, clutching his arm as I hold up his severed hand in my own to remove the ring. As I do, both the man and the hand crumble in on themselves like they are made of sand and can no longer hold their form. I drop the hand and watch as the fingers wiggle on the ground until they dissipate into dust.

The hairy humanoid howls and beats its chest, and the others rush past me into the corridors, fleeing.

Leela stands before me, holding the arm of a petite Djinni, whose hands remain shackled behind her. Her face and clothing are dirty, her dark curls disheveled. A shiny metal collar pokes out at her neck with a bloodred garnet inside. She looks terrified.

Immediately I crush the ring and the stone, and her collar falls at her feet, cracked down the center. Her bonds release and disappear as she whimpers.

"You're free," I say. "Leela will help you from here. But know you have support." I reach out to touch her arm, and she shies away. My heart breaks in that moment, remembering what it's like not to be able to trust the touch of another.

I turn to Leela. "You and I will discuss what you did later. One of these days, you will learn to trust me." I disappear before she can argue. I don't want to hear it.

21

THE BALANCE OF MAGIC

WHEN I GET HOME, I STRIP, SHOWER, AND THEN COLLAPSE ONTO MY BED to pull the blankets over my head. I don't know what time it is or care. There is far too much occupying my mind, and I'm afraid it just might burst at the seams if anything else happens. I may not need sleep, but the idea of being blissfully unaware of all my problems beckons me like a cup of cocoa on a winter's day.

I should have known it wasn't feasible.

Taj pulls the blankets back what feels like mere minutes later and shakes his head at me.

"I forgot to tell you it's done, didn't I?" I ask.

"I was worried sick until Leela showed up with a new Djinni and filled me in."

"Then why are you here?" I ask, sitting up to lean against the headboard.

"To check on my sister. I haven't heard much from you lately, and frankly that concerns me." He flops onto the bed beside me and tucks me under his arm.

I lean in, comfortable. "Thanks, but there's nothing to worry about. I have everything under control. The rest of the Djinn should be freed by...when's the thing?"

Taj cocks his head. "The curtain closure is planned for Friday night. This is what worries me."

"Just busy. I'm sure Leela won't let me forget."

"Something strange is going on with her too," Taj says, letting his head collapse against mine. "She's acting weird."

I grunt, feeling the pressure to give voice to the worries swimming in the back of my mind. "She's sick. She told me not to say anything, but you can say you noticed. I don't know what it is, but I worry that it has something to do with the prolonged effects of the lead they had her in for so long last year."

Taj sighs against me. "Fuck."

"Yeah. Shouldn't you go back to your boyfriend now?" I ask, pulling away and yanking the covers back up over me.

"We haven't finished yet, Mir. I'm afraid there's more."

I groan but wait for him to continue.

"Apparently you freed more than a Djinni."

I slip the covers off my face and bite my lip as I stare up at him.

"There was quite a scene at the Vatican. The reporters are guessing it to be an expensive movie hoax, like a marketing ploy the Pope somehow okayed. Not sure how that will hold up, but we'll see. In any event, there's a lot of buzz on the Internet now about magic being real." Taj examines his fingernails.

"You mad?" I ask, sitting again.

"Me? No. I find it utterly amusing. Humans learning about magic the hard way may be just what they deserve as long as it doesn't backfire and land Bigfoot back in a cage. That's what that huge thing was on camera, right?" He leans in as though interested in gossip.

I shrug. "I didn't ask. We just freed everyone."

"Well, one of the someones you freed has requested an audience with the Order. Apparently, she doubled back after you left and found Leela and sweet Irma."

So that was the petite Djinni's name. "And you want me present?"

"Actually she does. She's asked to speak to the one who destroyed her captor."

"I didn't mean to. I tore off his hand to get the stone. I was going to let the others decide what to do with him. He just...disintegrated."

"I suppose we should have anticipated something strange when we found it to be in the Vatican." Taj pats my knee through the blanket. "Pop on over when you're ready. Oh, and don't react too harshly. Dr. K is...a bit eccentric."

"Dr. K?" I furrow my brow.

"You'll see." Taj sings his answer as he fades away. I grumble and slide back under the sheets.

Friday night? We're closing the curtain that soon? My heart races, and I fling off the covers. May as well get this over with.

I snap, and I'm dressed in black jeans and a dark-blue sweater. I pull my fingers through my hair and transport myself over to Taj's apartment.

Cal answers the door in low-hanging pajama pants, which I'm beginning to suspect he wears all the time, and a white tee that hugs his sculpted chest. The frosted tips of his hair are perfectly mussed, and his green eyes glint in an amused way when he sees me. I suppose he's expecting a reaction, and he almost gets one when he steps aside to let me by.

Dr. K, or who I presume to be the doctor, looks more like a lizard than a woman, with blue scaly skin and a long tail that sweeps the floor as she paces, poking out from beneath her white lab coat. She wears oversized glasses perched on her snout, and a mop of curly yellow hair sits on top of her head like a wig.

She's wearing lipstick.

I blink away my initial thoughts and smile, extending a hand. "I'm Mira."

She smiles back, revealing sharp incisors, and shakes my hand with a surprisingly soft one of her own. Though her skin is ice cold.

"Dr. Emora Kingsley. Thank you for setting us free." Her voice carries a slight hissing sound beneath as her words drag out slowly.

I nod. "It's my job. Though, to be frank, I didn't know there were any other magical beings besides Djinn."

"That must have been quite a shock," she says as Cal passes behind me, closing himself and, I assume, Taj into their bedroom so we can talk.

"What can I do for you?" I ask, sitting on the arm of Taj's sofa.

"Ah, down to business. Of course. You must be quite busy. First you need to understand who and what I am. I started out human, you see. I worked for a foreign government as a scientist. I spliced my own DNA with that of an alien they'd taken into custody. This was the result." She gestures to her body.

I conjure a cup of tea and take a swig. It may be laced with a strong dose of vodka.

"Perhaps not the most innocent of people, I assumed that it was some form of divine justice when I was handed over to the Vatican for 'storage' in that place. Believe me, I'll never experiment unbidden on a living creature again."

"If you're looking for absolution, you came to the wrong person." I send my tea back into the ether.

"Hardly. I will have to live with my conscience for the rest of my life. I simply wanted you to understand my science background and perhaps my intellectual worth. You see, your companion, Leela, explained what the Order is. She also mentioned your plans for Friday night. Being a scientist, this concerned me greatly, but I recognized the fervor in her eyes. I've seen it in many a man before he became lost to his own dreams and agenda."

I swallow. I know what she means about Leela. It's why we all tiptoe so delicately around for her, unwilling to break what we sense is a fragile ego. But the truth is we've been the ones behaving weakly. "Go on."

She smiles again, broader, and I see some of her sharp bottom teeth overlap the top ones.

"I would very much like to study the phenomenon you label the 'curtain' between worlds and see if I can surmise its scientific effect."

I recall Rook's words in Paris—*I'd love to find someone trustworthy, willing, and able to do the research.* She could help both with hybrid knowledge and learning about the effects of closing the veil.

"Is there time?" I ask, leaning forward. "I'll give you whatever resources you need."

She nods. "I will do my best. Provide me with a laboratory and database with everything you know about your abilities and how they work. I've personally witnessed Irma and the effects of lead and the stone that controlled her. I believe it has to do with energy focal points and the way your energy is manipulated via particular mediums."

"It sounds like we are in good hands, Doctor." I stand and wave an arm overhead. She will find herself in exactly the setting she asked for, with a camera of course, so I can monitor her on my phone.

When I hear the giggling of children behind the couch, I shut my eyes tight in frustration. Every time I think I have a handle on things...

"Come out here." I point to the carpet at my feet.

Instantly Devon materializes before me along with a blushing Sophie, who, I hadn't realized until seeing her next to the lanky teenager, had stretched by almost a foot in height over the last year, her little girl features blossoming into more defined and mature angles, her large blue eyes being the most beautiful.

"Devon? Sophie? Where did you two come from, and how did you get here?"

"Devon came to find me," Sophie says, and she still sounds like the young girl with the high voice I know. "He told me what happened. Please don't be mad."

I press a finger to the crease between my eyes and collapse onto the couch. "Mad? Why would I be mad?" I manage to say it without sarcasm, or so I hope.

"We'd like to help Dr. K," Devon says, stepping forward.

I eye them suspiciously, a hand on my hip, sizing them up. Their auras run clear aqua. Between that and their eager faces, I can't help but relax. They are caught up in the excitement, and I can't well blame them.

"Fine," I say, trying not to smile as I pop us all over to the new lab.

An hour later, I head home, leaving the doctor with a strong impression of what will happen if she doesn't take perfect care of the two minor assistants. I've also made Devon call his grandmaman to let her know where he is and that he's safe.

When did my life become so complicated?

22

THREE HUNDRED YEARS AFTER ENSLAVEMENT

Wearing Kitra's family's scarlet-and-gold slave uniforms makes me feel only slightly better than being completely nude. I feel guilty missing the days when Taj would be up here dancing along with me despite the suggestive, undulating nature of the style our master always demanded. I wonder where he is now as I spin and contort, the thin layers of my skirt flowing out around me.

I've been passed along with my stone to Kitra's daughter and so on, always a female of the line. My current master goes by Amaya, but I'd never dare call her by anything other than Master. She's entertaining company tonight on the island she's had me transform in the ocean. With centuries of wealth and power come paranoia and exhausting magical demands.

Tonight she is entertaining a foreign dignitary of some sort, a man of power who has something she desires. He isn't any better than she is, so I don't feel the slightest guilt knowing she will likely have me take whatever it is she wants by force and kill him or freeze him in stone as she tends to favor. The macabre statues have been lining these halls since the first victim, Cephas.

But the dignitary in question has come accompanied by his own collection of servants and slaves, including several wives with beautiful ebony skin, darker than the night sky. It has not escaped my notice that not one of them has smiled or spoken a word. I don't even know if they speak his language.

One of his male servants with lighter skin like peaches and yellow in his hair keeps glancing at me from the back of the room where he sits on his knees awaiting his own master's call. His chest is bare, and the muscle shines beneath the lights from above.

When I catch his eye, his flesh burns red, and it is the most fascinating magic I've ever seen.

I feel my master's gaze on me at this moment, and I quickly adjust my own. But I do not like the curiosity in her eyes. I shiver but cover the action with a shimmy in my dance. Her attention is drawn back to her guest, who claps and whistles at the move, and I exhale with relief.

"Marvelous!" he says, and by the reaction of the wife seated beside him, he must have pinched her.

My heart breaks a bit for these wives of his, all trussed up in heavy chains of gold and silk, who cannot hide the sullen misery in their beautiful faces. At least I am called what I am, a slave. It is not hidden, though I, too, am trussed up in the red-and-gold colors of my master's house.

"Come down here, Mira."

My body obeys the command immediately and without question.

"She is lovely!" The dignitary is a small man with a wide face and dimpled brown skin. He wears a turban that is far too large for his head, but perhaps it is to add some illusion of height. He reaches out and squeezes my buttocks.

"Now, now, Mahmood," my master says, pulling me back toward her by my arm.

I do not let on that this surprises me. I assume she has some scheme in mind as she usually has no trouble with guests groping me.

"I mean no disrespect to you," he says immediately, arms spread as wide as his small girth will allow. Naturally he speaks to my master, not me, the one he has disrespected.

"Perhaps I can be convinced to allow you access to Mira for the evening." Ah, here it is. "But I must have guarantees that you will deal as I wish with the other tribes when it comes to trade arrangements."

"I am, of course, at your disposal," he assures, eyes drinking me in.

"Ah, but guarantees are something different." This cold statement draws Mahmood's attention. "I am not your average woman, Mahmood. I require certainties, and one night of pleasure with a slave, easily forgotten over time, guarantees no such thing."

"What is it you would have me do, then?" he asks.

"I will allow Mira to grant you three wishes, provided they do not undermine me in any way, if you sign a blood contract with me." My master takes a sip of wine, watching Mahmood's reaction over the lip of the goblet.

He pales and tugs at his collar. "A blood contract? Such an old custom. I thought those were stories."

Her crimson lips curl into a smile. "If it's a story, then you have nothing to fear."

I've created blood contracts for my masters in the past. I, too, had hoped they died with my last master, but alas, it seems she passed on the knowledge. Kitra created them. Anything that woman touched became laced with evil.

My master gives me a slight nudge, and I know what she wants. I step toward the man and run a finger along his arm and up to his shoulder, hovering at his neck. He shivers beneath my touch, even through his clothing, and he bites the tip of his tongue with a hiss.

"If you do not break the oath, nothing will happen," she continues. "You only have to fear the results if you seek to wrong me. You wouldn't do that, would you, Sheikh Mahmood?"

"My word is golden," he protests, puffing out his chest, which results in his ample stomach reaching much farther forward.

"It's decided then. Mira?" She does not have to utter the command. I will not risk the repercussions of defying her.

I extend my hand, and the sheikh tentatively places his inside. Sweat beads along his brow at the lip of his turban.

"I vow fidelity to you and your house for all time, Mistress Amaya." He says the words, pressing his eyes closed. I pull a dagger from the air and slice his palm, keeping firm hold of his hand, which glows beneath the magic of the vow.

In truth, neither the blood nor the glow are necessary, but Kitra demanded them as part of the theatrics she so enjoyed. Amaya reaches over and swipes some of the blood onto her finger, bringing it to her mouth and tasting it.

"It is done," she pronounces. "And I shall retire for the evening. Three wishes for the sheik, Mira. You know the rules. Enjoy."

I watch as she sashays away from the table, her own clothing swaying as she moves. When she has disappeared, Mahmood stands, as do all who accompany him. I lead the way to his guest chambers, knowing what is expected of me and wishing I could somehow fast-forward the evening so that I may file it away with all the others.

When we reach his rooms, he instructs his wives to retire for the evening as he will be spending it with me alone. I notice the pale manservant waits as silently and unobtrusively as possible in the corner. When all others have gone, he remains, and I wonder what his purpose is.

I do not have to wonder for long since he swiftly approaches as Mahmood throws out his arms. He removes the man's clothing for him, face dipped downward. Yet I notice him stealing glances at me, the same red color flushing his cheeks each time.

"Strip while dancing," Mahmood snaps at me. I assume that is not one of his wishes. I'd do otherwise, but I fear my master's wrath should he complain. So I comply.

I recall a time this would have undone me. Now it is an accepted part of my existence.

Somehow having the servant man present makes it harder, though, when the sheikh touches me. He keeps his eyes averted, however, during the act, which does not take more than a minute before the small man is satiated. Something about that touches me. It is a small dignity that I am not accustomed to.

"Now, about those wishes," Mahmood says, and I snap to attention.

"Yes, Master." It is how I am to speak to those of a high station so long as it does not usurp my real master. Some have tried. It does not end well for them.

"I wish for my body to be that of a strong and handsome man, and my stamina to be great as well. I'd like to be able to please my wives and others." He nods toward me as though offering me a great gift.

"As you wish." I snap my fingers, and his body morphs into a tall and muscular man. His appendage grows along with him, ready and at attention.

I glance toward the servant and find his eyes to be huge blue saucers. I've never seen eyes that color. I wonder if he is something closer to what I am with my own emerald irises.

Mahmood laughs delightedly and plucks me from the ground to swing me around in a circle of a dance. I hope he will not test this new body on me as I still do not find him attractive. I decide to distract him.

"Would you like to make your second wish?" I offer. Magic is the only thing more tempting to men than sex.

He sets me down, eyes glinting with possibility. He rubs his hands together as he contemplates.

"Two more wishes. I am already a rich man, but I wish to be powerful and feared by the other tribes so that no one will challenge me. That will make it easier to help your master," he adds the last as if to convince me.

"It is done," I say with a nod. "You will find you have a small army of powerful men to command when you return, as well as the reputation of someone not to be wronged." Whether he manages that appropriately remains to be seen.

"Splendid!" He laughs again.

"One more," I say. I must admit his enthusiasm is wonderful.

"Jude," he calls, and the servant man perks up, stepping forward immediately. "What should my last wish be?"

The man looks as shocked as I feel, and our eyes meet. "I am not certain I would be the best advisor, sir."

"Nonsense. Your people have a reputation for their cleverness. Shall I wish more money? More wives? Wait. I know." He turns toward me. "I wish for magic of my own."

My blood runs cold at his command. The only way I know how to gift this to him is not something I have ever done nor ever wish to do.

"What is the problem, woman?" he demands when I do not immediately comply.

"My apologies, Master. Your wish is...complicated."

I do not see the smack coming and fall onto the bed of colorful pillows. My hand flies to my face, and I notice Jude, muscles taut, fists clenched like he *wants to intervene but knows he can't. I shake my head at him as much as I dare.*

My eyes glow as I stand. If Kitra taught me one thing, it is to use theatrics to my advantage. "By granting that wish, I put my own master at risk." *Wind flies through my hair, whipping it into a frenzy.*

Mahmood stumbles backward and hides behind Jude's shoulder. Coward.

"I take it back!" *he screams.*

I let my eyes and hair settle and then offer a smile. "As you wish."

"I will contemplate my final wish and get back to you in the morning. Now leave me. Both of you. Jude, send in wife number one."

I bow and snap my fingers to replace my clothing and dart from the room. For now, I've escaped with more than I'd hoped, but I try not to think about what will happen if my master finds out what I've done.

23

FACING ROOK

LEFT WITH NOWHERE TO GO, I REALIZE I CAN NO LONGER STALL THE inevitable. I have to face him. He said he would give me time to think, and what I've done is avoid instead. Perhaps my approach is the problem. He said I can persuade, so instead of announcing my intentions, there is a way to teach him the truth about humanity. He's only experienced the best of it, after all. I've seen both the best and the worst.

I suck in a deep breath before knocking. As I begin to second-guess myself, his door swings open and Rook's beautiful face appears before me, amber eyes staring straight at me despite the fact he cannot see in the traditional sense. His long hair is loose and falls over his shoulders. He isn't wearing a shirt, and I long to reach out and touch the silken skin and trace his tattoos. But I keep my hands down by my sides.

"Hi," he says in his quiet voice, creating a yearning inside me to lean in and collapse against him.

"Hi." My voice comes out breathy.

He backs up, gesturing for me to come in, and I do, halting in his living room as he shuts the door. He turns and leans back against it, one bare foot pressed against the wood. He folds his arms across his chest, biceps bulging, and waits.

I clear my throat. "I, uh, I spoke to Alice, um, Daffodil."

He cocks his head.

"We had tea," I add.

"Okay," he says.

"It's hard for me to look at the positive, Rook." I walk toward him suddenly, unable to stay at such a distance. "I know it's what you want, what you're used to, but I've learned to be careful the hard way, and nothing is going to change that."

He reaches out and cups my cheek, brushing away a stray tear that I couldn't hold back. I lean into his touch and close my eyes.

"You don't know what it's like to be a slave, Rook. What these monsters are capable of. No." I press my fingers to his lips when he opens his mouth to speak. "I know they aren't the majority. We can argue about that as long as you like, but it doesn't matter. Even if there is one Kitra out there, and we accidentally unleash her unto this world..." I choke on the next words. I would rather die a thousand deaths than serve one more minute for someone like her.

"May I speak now?" he asks after a moment. It's a gentle request, and I nod in assent. "You're right. I can't begin to imagine the horrors you've endured. I must seem like a child to you in many ways. I admit when you told me your age, I hesitated. But my pull to you is so strong, Mira, that I can't stay away. The last two days have been like actual torture. I hear your thoughts, and when your voice isn't present, it's like a hole opens inside me. I don't know if you believe in fate, but I'm convinced you're mine."

I gasp, falling into his embrace. "I feel the same pull toward you." Admitting it feels silly and so unlike me. But with Rook, it's different from any of the others I've dared consider lovers. Rhada would have laughed at me and called me a hopeless romantic. Jude would have embraced me, but he thought of me as weaker as opposed to acknowledging my experience. Is it possible that this might actually be real? That Rook may remain and not be pulled from my grasp?

Dare I hope?

"I'm frightened," I admit, and he pulls away by an arm's length so he can tip my chin up to face him. "Every time I find joy, it has been fleeting and yanked from my grasp too quickly. Leaving Achan and others to use our blood for their own nefarious means...I just don't want to be responsible for that."

"I hear you," he says, and the words sink into my soul. I believe he does. I no longer try to hide my tears, but let them fall, fast and free. "I think I understand as best I can. But it kills me to see that part of you so beaten down. Don't let them take your hope, Mira. It's all we have left when the worst happens."

"I do believe in fate," I admit through sobs. "But I fear fate is only teasing me once again with something it will never let me have. It stands to reason that I deserve it all if fate is real."

Rook gathers me close and lifts me into his arms, carrying me to the sofa, so he can sit with me in his lap and hold me until my trembling subsides.

"Mira"—he lifts my chin again—"you never deserved the things that happened to you."

"How do you know?" I snort, yet I want him to tell me, to prove to me that it's true.

"I know because I know you. You love deeply, whether you recognize it or not. You are a protector of others. You care more than you let on. I hear you." He taps my head. "Sometimes the bad guys win because this is life, but my belief is that fate has a way of balancing it out in the end."

"If that's true, then perhaps I can hope for a future with you." I place my hands on his shoulders, and his smile is a gift like the rising sun.

"I love you, Mira."

No one has ever said it to me. Not in the way he means it. And the enormity of it both swells my heart to bursting and sends panic down my nerve endings. He loves me? How is that possible in such a short amount of time?

"I'll spend my life proving it to you if you let me," he says, clearly having heard my thoughts, and pulls me in for a kiss that curls my toes and chases the fear from my mind.

"What about the DB?" I ask, as we finally pull apart.

He considers. "We will figure out a compromise. It's what people who love each other do."

I place my hand over his heart, feeling the warmth and rhythm of its beat. He is the best of humanity. And perhaps the best of Djinn kind.

"Compromise," I repeat, unsure but willing to try. To trust him.

Then his lips are once again on mine, and the worries are abandoned as I sink into him, welcoming his velvet tongue as it sweeps against my own. He moans as I tangle my fingers in his hair and press my chest against his. I adjust my position by straddling his lap so that my knees rest on either side of him and his erection pushes through his thin pajama pants against my core.

I rub my body back and forth, rocking against him as my own pleasure rises. I need us both naked now, so I remove our clothes with a thought. He grunts, sliding against the slickness between my legs, no longer concealed behind layers of clothing.

"Whoa, Mira, slow down," he pants. "I want to pleasure you."

I speed up instead, pulling his hand up to cup my breast. "Pleasing me means being inside me because I need you now."

I adjust myself so that his tip grazes my opening, and every one of my nerve ending ignites into flame. I settle on him, taking his full length deep within, and thrust my hips forward, encouraging him to buck his body upward to meet my demand.

He doesn't disappoint, and as I climb toward a glorious crescendo, he reaches between us to circle his thumb over my nub, sending me into the stratosphere with an explosion of pleasure that momentarily blinds me. My muscles clench around him, and he joins me in utter ecstasy, holding my hips firmly down on him as he empties his seed into my spasming body.

I collapse against him, burying my face in the crook of his neck and nipping at his salty skin. "I love the feel of you inside me."

"Being inside you is my favorite place to be," he agrees.

I jiggle against him as I laugh, accidentally eliciting renewed shock waves of pleasure where he remains, slowly softening.

A buzzing sounds from somewhere off to the right where I sent our clothing. With a groan, I release him and sit on the couch beside him as he rises to retrieve the phone from his pants. At least I can admire the view of his perfectly pert bottom when he stoops to collect it.

His brow furrows as he checks the screen. "Not mine." He dives back into the pile to retrieve my phone from my pants pocket and tosses it to me.

I barely ever pay attention to the thing. I almost forgot I even remembered to stick it in my pocket this morning. Perhaps Taj's nagging has finally gotten to me.

A quick glance sends my heart sputtering. "It's from Doctor K. She has information and wants to meet with me already."

"Dr. K?" Rook asks.

I magic us back into our clothes as I explain. "You want me to include you from now on, then here's your chance. Come with me."

Rook returns my smile and takes my offered hand so I can blink us over to the doctor's laboratory.

24

THE MAGIC CIRCUIT

THE LABORATORY I CREATED FOR THE DOCTOR IS ON AN ISLAND. I SUPPOSE they are my specialty when I need an off-the-radar place. But this time it's in the warm waters of the Pacific that I fly. The building itself is a dome-shaped structure, filled with the latest tech as well as the comforts of a lavish lifestyle. It's what I'm used to supplying, but at least this time it was my own gift, not a command fulfilled.

We appear inside the domed top. Sleek silver machinery surrounds us, along with several leather chairs on rollers, three of which are filled by the doctor and her two young assistants. Sophie rolls over to me immediately, clearly using magic to propel herself across the vast room.

"Hi, Auntie Mira." She considers Rook at my side and smiles. "Hello, Rook."

I am taken aback and turn to him, wondering if he's the one who knew more than he let on. But he seems just as perplexed.

It only lasts a heartbeat though before his face melts, and he grins back. "Hello, Sophie, nice to meet you." He turns to me with a wink. "We can hear each other."

That explains it, and it isn't a mystery if she was gifted with his blood in utero.

Her face falls, and I realize she heard what happened to her from

Rook. But before I can say a word, he drops to his knees by her side and takes her hand. In that moment, he is more of a father than Achan ever was.

I don't know what he says to her, as I cannot hear it, but she soon flings herself into his arms and they hug, his face lighting up over her shoulder until she releases him.

"Hello, Devon," I say to the curious boy watching from beside the doctor.

"*Bonjour*," he replies with a smile that reveals dimples I've never seen before on him. Lovely.

"Thank you for coming so quickly," Dr. K says, rising from her own chair, which follows behind her as her tail is caught in the space between the back and the seat. She doesn't seem to notice or care, so I try to ignore it.

"Please tell me what you've learned."

"I'm afraid it's as I suspected," she says, grimacing as best she can with a long snout. "To put it in layman's terms, if you close the door or curtain between dimensions, you will effectively be stopping the complete circuit from being created."

"Circuit?" I ask, stepping closer.

"Yes. If you think of your 'magic' as energy, then you can picture it flowing along a circuit of sorts. That's where you access it and manipulate it."

Makes sense. Magic is essentially energy manipulation.

"So if you interrupt that circuit, the energy can't flow, and then poof. Nothing." She uses her hands to make an exploding gesture.

"What does that mean?" I am so close now that I am practically in her face. I feel Rook's presence at my shoulder.

"It means anything created from that energy will no longer have a source to draw from and will cease to exist."

My mouth dries up. Rook takes over the questioning.

"Does that mean the Djinn themselves will vanish?"

"No, I believe their bodies will hold, but then age naturally as a human."

"So it's like Leela said. We will lose our powers?" I ask.

"Yes, but it's more than that." Dr. K gestures to follow her to a monitor where she can demonstrate. "I've set up this simulation. Those green dots are Djinn, and the magic is this circle of energy that passes through each of them. These blue dots are magicians. The red are other spells or creations made from magic." She points to blue and red dots that are all outside the circle of energy.

"Now watch what happens when I interrupt the circuit." She presses a button, and the circle disappears. The green dots fade into yellow, which I assume is human. The blue dots blink and become yellow as well. The red dots blink and then vanish completely.

"So the magicians will also be turned human," I say, trying to make sense of it.

"Correct," Dr. K says. "But it's the red dots who are alive that worry me most."

"Red dots who are alive?" I echo, not understanding. Rook clutches my shoulder, and I hear Sophie gasp from somewhere behind me.

"We're the red dots," Sophie says, and I spin to find her shrunken into her seat, looking like the tiny girl I met two years ago, trembling in fear. Only this time it's not caused by me.

"The hybrids—" Understanding dawns.

"We are a direct creation of magic," Rook says.

"Aren't we all?" I ask, still confused and beginning to panic. "If we and the magicians turn yellow, then they should too."

"Sadly, no," Dr. K says. "You are beings, and the bodies you think you created are your actual form here in this dimension. This is how you would exist here, even unaided by magic. Magicians would exist without the magic that altered them, leaving them in their regular human bodies. But hybrids, as you call them, well, they would not exist on their own without the help of magic."

"And people like me, who've been saved by Djinn blood, would revert to our original setting," Devon adds quietly. "So I'll be sick again."

I rush to pull him into my arms. The action is so automatic that I hardly register it. I don't point out that he appears to be a hybrid now as well. Either way, it's not a good situation.

"We can't allow this to happen." I utter it as a command toward the doctor, who spreads her hands wide in a helpless gesture.

"Then don't initiate it."

I picture Leela's face when I inform her that her grand plans cannot happen. It isn't a pretty picture. The last thing I want to do is break my friend, my sister.

Is this fate's last laugh? Is my vision of it real, while Rook's remains too glossed by his rose-colored glasses? Has he been given to me only to be taken away?

"No," he says, gently tugging me up and into his arms. "We can stop it from happening. Together."

I bury my face in his shoulder, not wanting to allow the doubts that already cloud my mind.

"They won't hurt Sophie," I say instead. Taj loves her. Jered loves her. No, they won't allow this. I have nothing to worry about.

"See?" Rook soothes. "It'll be okay, Mira."

I remember with vivid clarity the last time those words were spoken to me by a lover.

It didn't end well.

25

THREE HUNDRED YEARS AFTER ENSLAVEMENT

I LINGER IN THE HALL AS JUDE RUSHES TO RETRIEVE WIFE NUMBER ONE. SHE glances resentfully at me as she's escorted into her husband's rooms. I suppose she thought she had a reprieve for the night. Perhaps she'll at least appreciate the improvements. At least he wished specifically to be able to give his wives pleasure.

Jude bows himself backward out of the chambers, shutting the double doors before him and then straightening with a heavy sigh. When he turns and finds me watching, he blushes again.

"Pardon me," he says and turns to go.

"Please don't leave," I say, my words echoing in the space of the silence as he pauses, his back to me in midretreat.

He spins to face me, surprise written on his face, which I now see is spattered with small brown spots across his nose. I find it oddly attractive.

"How may I be of service, milady?" he asks with a sweeping bow.

I am so stunned that I take a step back, looking around me. "Are you speaking to me?" I finally ask.

He laughs lightly. "Yes, of course."

"I am no lady. I am Djinn and a slave."

He frowns, his shoulders dipping. "You look like a lady to me. And if it were up to me, you'd be treated as such. I apologize for what my master did."

He won't look in my eyes when he says it, and that makes me feel awkward and small.

I wave it away. "I am expected to allow it. I got over it a long a time ago." I haven't really, but I should have, I'm certain.

"Do you ever have free time to yourself?" he asks suddenly.

"Like now?"

He laughs again. "I suppose so. Would you care to accompany me as I walk? My own master will not expect me to return until dawn."

"I will not be expected until then as well. My master will assume I am still in there." I nod toward Mahmood's rooms.

Jude offers his hand, and I take it. He leads the way down the winding stone steps to the main level but pauses as if he doesn't know where to go.

"Would you like to see my favorite spot?" I offer.

"I'd love that."

We chat as we walk, and I find myself fascinated by the details of his culture and life.

"So you are a slave as well?" I ask, leading him up another staircase toward the tower that is my destination.

"Yes, I was taken from my home when our village was conquered. We were technically part of Greece, but a rather far outlier. I doubt they even realize we've been invaded. My brother was killed fighting, and I laid down my sword. So you see, you are spending your precious free time with a terrible coward."

I pause at the landing outside the balcony. "I don't think that's cowardice. The desire to live isn't something to be ashamed of."

His smile is genuine. "Thank you, Mira. That means a lot from a brave Djinni like you."

I laugh. "How am I brave?"

"You faced down my master when he wished for magic. Forgive me for my assumption, but I would venture to guess you lied at least partially about being able to grant him that."

I avert my gaze and flip my ponytail over my shoulder. "Please do not tell him or my master. I could not bear to do what he asks."

"I won't tell, don't worry. I just saw your hesitation. If it was given that you could not accommodate him, there would have been no pause."

"You truly are clever," I say, looking up. "I am glad your master is not."

"What is it you are afraid to do?" he inquires.

I hesitate. "To become a magician, you have to ingest the blood of a Djinni."

Jude recoils. "I see. I cannot blame you then. If I may make a humble suggestion, though. Next time, offer a relic of some sort that has magic for him to wield."

My eyes widen with surprise. "That's a wonderful idea. Thank you. Now, pay attention. I want to see the full effect of this view."

I push open the door to the balcony, and the freezing air kisses my skin. I close my eyes momentarily to the rush of the wind, enjoying the fresh air from the sea. Then I open them to take in my favorite view in the world. The grand expanse of never-ending stars painted across the night sky.

From the edge of the balcony, with the rush of the ocean below, I feel as though I am once again free floating in the universe beyond.

Jude brushes next to me, skin prickled with bumps from the chill air. His teeth chatter slightly as he looks out beyond the horizon, eyes wide with wonder that makes my belly warm.

I take his freezing hands in mine and send a coat of warmth over him. It was rude of me to forget about his human frailty when it comes to temperature.

"Thank you," he says softly, rubbing his thumb over my fingers tenderly. A small shock of excitement tingles to life and travels up my arm and over my body at his touch. It's something I haven't felt in a very long time.

"If you had three wishes, what would they be?" I ask. My master has had me grant so many for others. It would be nice to offer something of my own free will. Something I forget existed at all until this moment.

He sucks in a breath. "Are you offering?"

I nod, eager to please this new...friend.

He sighs and lets my ponytail slide through his fingers as he thinks. "Mira, I don't think you can give me what I want."

"What is it?"

"Freedom. My home back. My family." The words cause him pain. I see it in his eyes that reflect in the moonlight. He presses his fingers to my mouth before I can respond. "I'm not asking for them. I wish I could wish for your *freedom as well, but I know the only one with the power to make real wishes of you is your master. The world is a cruel place. But I do have a request if you will hear me out."*

"Yes," *I say, disappointed in knowing his words to be truth.*

"Would you permit me to kiss you?"

I nearly laugh. "Of course. That wish I can grant easily."

Jude leans in and presses his lips to mine, at first light like the stroke of a feather, then harder, stealing my breath as he traces the line of my lips with his tongue. I open to him, curious about the flutterings in my belly, and we explore each other fully, embracing beneath the stars.

"I wish there were a softer place to lie you down and show you what a real lover should be," *he says as I kiss my way down his neck, enjoying the sweet and salty taste of him.*

"Perhaps there is a place where I can show you things you've never experienced." *I smile, and we float into the night sky, high above the island fortress where nothing but stars surround us.*

Jude pulls me in, our bodies pressed together so that I feel his desire grow. "This is indeed something I have not experienced," *he says, letting a hand cup my breast above my top.* "Is this all right?"

I blink, and our clothing waits on the balcony beneath us. "Yes, but this is preferable."

His mouth covers mine again as his hands rove over my body, exploring each secret crevice and sensitive spot. He plucks at my nipple as though he is playing a musical instrument, and more pulses of desire awaken, lower than my belly this time. His other hand cups my bottom, and he slips his fingers farther between my legs to stroke at the crease of my lower lips.

"Mmm," *I murmur, throwing my head back in delight as he explores, taking my nipple in his mouth and curling his tongue around the hardened nub, flicking it and sending waves of pleasure through me.*

Lazily, I drop my hand down to feel the length and weight of him, sliding my thumb over his sensitive tip and then gliding my fist up and down over him, enjoying the moans it draws from his lips.

He turns me around in midair so that my back is against him and holds me tight, one hand on my breast, the other between my legs, working against my clit in circles drawn faster and faster as I thrust my hips against the mounting pleasure. I moan as he draws the climax from me and then angles himself to drive inside me from behind. I lean forward, allowing him access, and he glides inside the warm, slick opening, throbbing with desire for his presence. Using my hips as handholds, he thrusts inside me, losing himself to an almost animal rhythm as he drives in hard and fully each time, working me up once again to the promise of a long-awaited and much-needed climax. When I call out, it's a trigger for him to release his own pleasure that he's held onto admirably for so long. When he finishes, I twist toward him, face-to-face and body to body. I kiss him again, this time taking it slow and deep as I float us back to the ground.

We dress in silence, smiles on our faces. And when I turn to him again, he tucks a stray hair behind my ear, caressing my cheek.

"I may be a slave for the rest of my life, but I've done something only the angels have been blessed to do until now. Thank you, Mira."

"Thank you for your attention." I exit the balcony with Jude trailing behind and wind my way down to the kitchens to wait until daybreak or my master's call.

Jude has granted me a wish of my own whether he knows it or not. A night solely for myself.

26

CEREMONY CRASHER

"WHAT DAY IS IT?" THE BOTTOM OF MY STOMACH DROPS OUT.

"Friday," Sophie says, furrowing her small brow.

Shit. "What time is it?" I demand of the room at large.

"It's seven p.m. here," Devon replies, checking his cell phone.

Why the fuck do I not pay attention to these things? I do the calculations in my head.

"We have to go. Now." I grab Rook's hand and scoop Sophie's into my other one. "Hang on tight." I tell them.

I speed through space, slowing time as I rush for the circle of Djinn. I really need to pay more attention to dates and times.

"Hold!" I shout, materializing in the center of the circle.

The voices of Djinn rise in a jumble of confused muttering. Our appearance has caused a stir. As long as it's not too late.

"What's with the dramatic entrance?" Taj asks, leaning forward but not breaking the circle by dropping hands with Cal. I grow braver in his presence, knowing he will hear me out and see reason.

"You have to listen to me." I use his trick of projecting a booming voice out across the expansive circle. They all must hear the truth. "You cannot close the veil."

"You have no right!" Leela screams, and everyone else falls silent.

I've had enough of Leela's twisted mission. I will not allow her care-lessness to harm those I love. I need her to hear me. She has to process my words, so I speak low and even, staring into her eyes and daring her to ignore me.

"You did not heed my words once before, and it cost too much. You will hear me this time, Leela. I told you there were too many unknowns."

"If this is a way to get even—"

"No. This is to save the one I love and the ones you love, Leela. If you close that veil, then Sophie dies." I steal a glance at Rook and squeeze his hand. This isn't the way I should have declared my love, but every word is true. I can see in his smile that he understands.

"Sophie?" Jered says, his face pale. If Leela won't hear me out, he will. I focus on him.

"It's true," Sophie says, and more murmurs break out.

"How is that even possible?" Leela hisses. "She's a magician like Jered."

"She's more than a magician," I say.

Taj glares at me in warning, but I can't hold back. It's the only way. So I look him in the eyes as I say it.

"She's part Djinn."

Now the others erupt in chaos. Hands drop and the circle breaks. Taj clears his throat as though it's done through a megaphone and speaks over everyone.

"Clearly Mira has information that must be considered before we make any rash decisions. A decade is nothing to us. We will reconvene in the near future. Thank you all."

"No!" Leela shrieks, but Jered holds her back in his arms as she flails forward in hysterics, face crimson and spittle flying from her mouth.

It feels like someone is wringing out a wet cloth in the middle of my chest. I watch, unable to take my eyes off her as Jered whispers into her ear, calming her. But the arrows she shoots through her eyes land square in my heart.

Rook grips my hand, and so does Sophie, though I see Taj taking hold of her on the other side. Some of the Djinn move off elsewhere, and some hover nearby, waiting to gather more information no doubt. Cal comes over to join our smaller group as well, but I can't stop watching Leela crumble.

She'll never forgive me for this. That hurts, but I suppose it's karma since I had so much trouble forgiving her for so many years. It's much easier to blame another person when the truth is it's far more complicated.

I will have to be that person. I will take the brunt of her anger if it means saving the man I love.

The man I love.

I reel from the words. Not only am I in love again, but this time, he also loves me. I guess Rhada did in her own way, but now I know the difference.

A warm tear slides down my cheek as Leela finally collapses into sobs, shuddering against her lover's chest.

"I will explain everything, I promise," I say to Taj and Cal. "But I had to stop it first. Please come with me to see Dr. K. She'll show you the evidence."

Taj swallows, his Adam's apple bobbing in his throat as he glances toward Leela. He nods. "You should come too, Jered. Lee."

Jered's face is also covered in tears. "I think I better take Leela home first."

"No!" she shouts, pushing away from his chest with her fists. "I want to know what this is about."

He nods his assent, and I beckon them to follow us. Jered should be fine as long as he keeps hold of her, and frankly she needs him to do so.

We materialize back at the laboratory, and I conjure a sofa in the shape of a semicircle for everyone as well as a bottle of water. Taj's mouth drops open as Devon jumps up and rushes to join us, somehow fitting himself into the small space between myself and Sophie.

I can't help but notice Leela's breathing as her chest pumps up and down in a pattern far too fast.

"Welcome," Dr. K says, strolling up to join us in the open part of the semicircle, her tail dragging behind on the tile floor. "I assume Mira has shared the situation."

"Not at all," Leela says. "All she did was wait till the last moment and dramatically shut down what I've worked over a year toward."

"Allow me to explain then," Dr. K says with a worried glance in my direction. She launches into the same explanation she gave to us.

"I don't understand," Jered says when she finishes. "Who are these hybrids, and why would Sophie be considered one? Her father is a magician, and her mother is a human."

"I'm one," Rook says, keeping my hand entwined with his and in his lap. "And I'm afraid it's my fault that Sophie is one as well." He calmly explains what Achan did as the others listen with barely concealed repulsion.

Taj buries his face in his hands.

"It's a lie," Leela says.

"No." I sit up straight, drawing in a deep breath. "I went to see Achan and confirmed everything."

"Then he's lying! How dare you free him, even for a moment?" She stands, pointing a finger at me as sparks fly out of the tip.

I rise to meet her, releasing Rook's hand with some difficulty. "He wasn't lying. I am one hundred percent positive. The fact is, Rook remembers him as well. And you never have to worry about my freeing him again. Not any of them. They're gone. Forever." I may as well lay all my cards on the table. I don't like hiding things and know it's better to get the truth out sooner rather than later.

Leela pales and stumbles backward. Jered is up like a lightning bolt and catches her just as she swoons into his arms, eyes fluttering closed.

Everyone else stands as well as Jered lays his unconscious lover on the sofa, kneeling at her side.

"What happened?" he asks, frantically searching our faces. "Was there lead? You seem okay."

"No lead," Taj says, kneeling beside him to examine her.

I step backward into Rook's solid body. Was I too harsh? I forgot about her condition, but it's as Jered strokes her hair so lovingly that an idea forms in my head. I blink as the realization hits. And one moment of searching with my enhanced senses confirms my suspicion.

"Jered," I call. I repeat myself louder a moment later when he ignores me.

He turns with questions in his eyes.

"She's okay, but you're both going to be very glad you didn't close that curtain."

"I already am, and I'm sure she will be as well when she realizes that Sophie really was in danger," he says.

I suck in my bottom lip, not knowing if I should talk to her first, but my question is answered when Leela stirs, and consciousness seeps back in. Taj helps her to sit up on the couch. I move over to them and kneel beside Jered.

"Lee, honey," I say and am met with a death glare, which I ignore. "You know how you haven't been feeling well lately?"

"I asked you not to say—"

"Is this true?" Jered interjects.

I wave him off with my hand. "I know. But now I know what it is, and you are going to need to be honest." I place a hand flat on her stomach.

She stares at it for a minute, brows furrowed.

"It's rare to conceive a Djinn hybrid, but we know it's easier when the magician and Djinni are in love. That's how Rook was born."

I sit in silence as understanding sinks in.

"I'm *pregnant*?" she whispers.

Jered sits back on his heels, eyes wide.

"Congratulations?" I shrug.

The silence is broken by Sophie's squeals as she tackles Jered and then Leela with hugs and excited babbling about the baby.

Tears swim in Leela's eyes as she gazes at Jered, hand splayed across her stomach. "Our love created a life?"

Jered's smile couldn't be wider as he covers her hand with his own. I watch in awe as his blossoming purple aura seeps over and through her, melding with the unmistakable greenish glow from the child's. Now that I've searched and found it, it's so clear to me.

Rook encircles me with one arm, pulling me aside to give them some space, and I back away, gaze still locked on the joyous couple. When Jered leans in to whisper in her ear, I finally break away to find Taj and Cal also locked together, eyes brimming with tears of joy. It's a magical moment, and I suspect one I will not likely forget.

In fact, it's moments like these that make my long existence worth living, I realize, leaning my head on Rook's shoulder. Had this happened a month ago, the acute awareness of not having a partner would have brought pain instead of joy. With that realization, some of the fear of impermanence lightens, and it's like a physical weight falls from my shoulders.

I don't realize that I too am crying until Rook wipes some of the moisture from my face. Without him, I never would have figured out hybrids exist. We would have closed the curtain and snuffed out so many lives. The thought of losing him takes my breath away.

"There's something I wanted to do after the curtain was closed," Jered says, breaking the spell. "But now, well, I think this is even better."

He holds out a hand, and a small velvet box materializes in his palm. Somewhere behind me, Sophie squeals again.

"Leela, you are my life and my love. I want to spend every minute of the rest of my life with you. Please, marry me."

Taj gasps a little and presses the back of a fist to his mouth.

Leela's eyes have never looked so big as Jered opens the box and reveals a beautifully understated ring made of silver with an infinity sign woven into it.

"I didn't think you'd want any diamonds or anything." He rubs his free hand along the back of his neck and blushes.

We collectively hold our breath as Leela sits, still and silent, staring at the delicate offering.

"I...I...I..." We all lean forward, waiting for the yes to slip from her lips and seal their happily ever after.

"I have to go."

Leela vanishes, and Jered is left on his knees, holding a ring.

27

SISTERS

"I MAY MURDER THAT GIRL," TAJ SAYS AFTER A MOMENT.

"I'll go," I volunteer, slipping out of Rook's arms. I can't stand to watch Jered's heart break any further, though I'm not sure I can hold back my anger any more than Taj.

I find her in a palm tree on an island not far from the laboratory. She sits on the top, plucking at the giant leaves and staring off into the undulating waters of the Pacific. The salty air carries a different scent than the lake where we've settled, and I can't help but inhale it, allowing it to soothe my frustration with Leela.

I pop in next to her, an arm extended around her stiff shoulders. She continues on exactly as if I hadn't done it, confirming I am perhaps the last person she wanted to see.

"I'm sorry it couldn't be done," I say, staring out at the ocean with her. I mean it.

"Last year," she begins softly, "I was ready to die. I'd lost everything not once, but twice. I learned that things can always get worse and that they'll never stop coming for us or our happiness." She wipes at her face with her arm.

I wait.

"Then this miracle happened. I had a shred of hope that I could stop them from coming. That I could live the life I always wanted with the man who made me feel like a real person. I should have known it was false hope. It's always false."

She throws a kernel from the tree, and we watch it arc high and land several meters away from shore in the water.

"There was a miracle," I say, smoothing her hair. "But it wasn't the one you expected."

She lets out a sharp laugh that shakes her entire body. "You're going to tell me our love is beautiful and we've created a child and what could be better?" She finally turns to face me, eyes glowing green, not from power, but from tears. "Now I'm responsible for bringing a child into this, Mira. A child who will be hunted and used. A child made of love, yes, but deserving of a life of freedom without worry of being a slave!"

Leela dissolves into tears, collapsing against me in a shuddering, wet heap. I do my best to hold her as she falls apart, stroking her hair and back, kissing the top of her head. When she quiets, I continue to stroke her as I speak, watching some pelicans swoop down into the water to catch fish.

"Or maybe this child is a fresh start because now we all have more knowledge and understanding of the world and what it holds, both beauty and danger. We also have something now that we didn't have then, not really."

Leela peers up at me.

"We have each other. We know what it means to be a real family now, Lee. You are my sister, and I will never turn my back on you again, even if it means hurting you to do so."

My own tears slide down to mix with hers as she embraces me, and we rock back and forth in each other's arms on the top of the tree to the roar of the ocean and the call of birds.

"Jered loves you," I say. "He wants a chance at that life that you're afraid to live. Don't disappoint him. If you don't try, then they've already won."

"How can I do it, Mira? How can I live like I'm not terrified of every moment to come? Every sound, every sudden movement, terror seizes me that my time is up." She squeezes my arms so tight that it's painful.

"I don't know the answer to that," I admit as she searches my face. "It's something I have to work on as well. But maybe with each other for support, those thoughts will lessen. Maybe we will eventually be able to live in the moment and enjoy the happiness as it comes. I have a feeling this little one will help."

Her face hardens again as she pulls back. "It's easy to say that, isn't it? You don't know what it's like, fearing that any moment someone who depends on you could be taken."

I flinch. "I've lost more loved ones than you realize." I stop before more words come pouring out, ones I'll regret if I speak them aloud. I blamed her enough when it was never her fault. But the fact she thinks so little of me and my own feelings comes as a blow, and I won't pretend it doesn't hurt.

"I didn't mean to imply otherwise," Leela says, staring down at a piece of a palm frond in her hand. "I know you've lost. I just mean... Jered's here, and so is this child. You can't possibly imagine the weight of that responsibility."

"Maybe not as the one carrying it, but I'm going to love and protect that child with my life. Don't you know that? You are the mother, yes. But we are a family, and that baby"—I sniff, trying to hold back my emotions—"is one of us."

Leela looks up at me and the fierceness I know is in my face even as I tremble with too many emotions to name, and I see something mirror that in her as her drive for survival returns.

"You're right, Mira. We have each other's backs."

"That's why they may have taken you again a year ago, but now you sit here free with the man you love waiting for you to return to his arms...and his proposal." I shove her arm lightly.

"Poor Jered!" Leela straightens like she's just realized what she's done. Then she pops out of the tree, leaving me shaking my head.

28

IN THE BEGINNING

MY ONE-NIGHT AFFAIR WITH JUDE TURNS INTO A MONTH OF STOLEN MOMENTS and desires fulfilled in the shadows of the palace. Our masters have hatched a plan to bring the other tribal heads here to be shown exactly what awaits them in terms of reward or punishment. For some reason, I find it more diffi-cult to perform my master's wishes when Jude sits silently on his knees, watching.

"Ahmed here seems to feel disinclined to bow, Mira. Show everyone what happens when they choose unwisely."

I raise my hands, willing my eyes to glow as I know she prefers. It's about the fear we instill, she instructed me once, and I knew her mother would be proud. The man stands defiant, proudly jutting his chin so that his curly beard lifts in its entirety in an almost absurd way. I force him to his knees before me as he spits and swears about a woman daring such things. Then comes the bone-crunching pressure on his fingers, followed by his wrists, his arms, and so on. When I reach his shoulders, I pause and catch sight of Jude's usually impartial mask. The horror in his eyes is clear, and I falter, continuing to apply pressure as commanded while shame bubbles through me. I thought that had been squashed out of me long ago at the hands of Cephas.

My master grins at the expression of pain frozen on Ahmed's face, clear pleasure at his sudden silence and inability to protest shines through her very pores. She licks her lips, and I imagine her savoring the moment of complete unraveling between pain, disbelief, and acquiescence. Then she lifts her own hand to urge me forward, and I close my eyes as I finish the job, crushing his bones one by one until his consciousness fades away.

I leave him alive because she has not given me the signal for death. I learned to pay attention to a master's body language years before this one was born, having been beaten within an inch of my life with a lead rod for misunderstanding Kitra's wishes and putting a victim out of his misery before she was ready.

This time, I suppose it has to do with him begging her to allow him to change his mind before the others, who are already visibly terrorized. She will have me kill him, but she wishes him to break before his peers first. She would never leave a human servant alive when they have defied her once, especially where she cannot keep a constant eye on them.

When I open my eyes again, the man's servants have dragged him away from the front of the throne and Jude's mask has once again fallen into place.

When it is time to retire for the evening, Amaya requests the presence of the youngest and most handsome of the sheikhs. When she sees him ogling me, she tells me my presence will not be needed this evening and to be sure that each of the other heads of tribe is secured in their rooms. In other words, lock them in so they cannot talk among themselves or gather.

When I have done as she requires, I make my way toward the dungeon, though it is my least favorite place on the island. I am not yet ready to face Jude after what he witnessed. Of course I can explain, but when I try to think of what words to use, exhaustion seeps into my bones, and my throat grows dry and blocked. I don't want to explain myself. I don't even want to be myself.

I conjure a comfortable bed for the evening in the middle of the hall outside the cells and lie down to rest. I'm not tired, and I would love to go up and look at the stars, but I am too afraid he will be there.

When he appears in the corridor at the bottom of the circular stairway, I am startled into a sitting position, heart beating so hard I feel it in my temples. His face betrays nothing but concern, yet all I see was the horror of that one moment.

I glance at my hands against the velvet covers.

"You are avoiding me?" he asks, and I feel him move closer, not quite touching the bed.

"I know what you saw today, and that no matter how I try to explain, you cannot truly understand the extent of my situation." My heart grows heavy, and tears build behind my eyes. I am practiced, though, and I do not allow them to fall.

He sits, the bed depressing with the weight of it. One of his hands, calloused and dry, covers my own.

"Mira, I know what it's like to be a slave. But the power you have...you're right. I cannot begin to understand what she's done to make you feel you have no choice—"

My head jerks up to face him, and by the way he cowers, I assume my eyes are glowing with shock and anger. "Choice? You think this is in any way a choice?" My voice grows shrill, and Jude yanks his hand back.

"I didn't mean to upset you." I watch his face, my heart sinking as I realize his words are motivated by fear and not love.

I swallow back my anger as best I can. I knew this would happen. Perhaps it's best not to avoid it any longer. I shake my head, trying to find the right way of explaining it. But he takes my silence as invitation.

"I know it can feel like we have no say, and it may well be best not to defy our masters for fear of retribution. But if I had power like yours..."

I clench my jaw, unwilling to snap at him. He doesn't understand. Why would he?

"If you had power like mine"—I cup his cheek in my hand—"then you would wear one of these." I let my finger trail over the ruby in my choker.

Jude's eyes narrow as he stares at it.

"I am bound by magic to the matching stone in my master's control. She is a magician, and I have been passed to her from her ancestors. I have no choice but to obey her commands. I can try to fight it but will never succeed. Believe me, I've tried."

Jude's sharp intake of breath lets me know he may finally comprehend at least part of the danger I pose. The lost cause I am.

"There must be a way to defy her. A magical answer perhaps?" He grasps my hands and presses them to his lips.

"There is nothing. Not even hope." Hope is dangerous.

"I will never give up on you, Mira," he promises, and I shudder to think what will happen if we are found out.

"You should," I admonish. *"Stay safe, Jude. Stay away from me, and do not attempt to help. I promise if it were possible, I'd have done so by now."*

In answer, he pulls me in for a kiss. But I cannot return his passion tonight, and I pull away.

"I'm sorry," I say and wave a hand, sending him back upstairs to his master's door.

If hope is dangerous, then love hurts worse than torture.

29

A MEETING OF THE MINDS

By the time I arrive, Leela has tackled Jered to the ground, and they are kissing. I notice the ring fitting snuggly on her finger. Taj's arm brushes my own, and I glance over at him as Rook puts a hand on my opposite shoulder.

"We need to talk," Taj whispers.

I nod as he slips his hand in mine, and the three of us—Taj, myself, and Rook—transport back to Taj's apartment where he sits, crossing his legs on the leather sectional, a martini in hand, overflowing with olives. I understand his need for a drink, so I say nothing.

Taj narrows his eyes, dragging his gaze over Rook. "You're familiar."

"He filled in for the bouncer when we went to the club that night." I grab Rook's hand, partially in support and partially for support.

Taj grins wickedly, forcing me to blush. Thankfully he says nothing else about our relationship. Instead he dives right into the crux of the matter.

"So we can't close the veil. I won't lose Sophie, even theoretically. This news also complicates matters because we have a new class, as it were, to deal with. Aside from Sophie, and present company of course, they could represent a threat. Your magic is stronger than a typical magician. In truth, you can do things even we Djinn cannot." Taj pops an olive in his mouth as he watches Rook for a reaction.

"The danger isn't posed by what I am, but who I am inside. That's true of all of us," Rook says, and pride brings a smile to my lips.

"Even Djinn can choose poorly," I add. "Brolach?" I feel bad when Taj visibly winces at the name and the reminder that he trusted the Djinni serial killer. But what Rook said was true. Anyone can be evil. And anyone can be good. "Jered and Sophie versus Achan and Kitra."

"Fair enough," Taj says before I find any more painful comparisons. "So we continue on as before then, finding and freeing any enslaved Djinn."

I draw a deep breath and release Rook's hand to sit on the arm of the sectional. From this vantage point, I am able to see both men. "There is another way to help us integrate so that the danger lessens over time."

Rook beams at me, and it gives me all the courage I need to continue.

"We are mingling with humans. The hybrids are the result. If we were to make this knowledge and magic in general available to the masses, then it won't be a coveted secret anymore. It will be common-place and accepted."

I cannot believe I've said it. But now that I have, I know I'm right. Rook is right.

Taj, on the other hand, nearly spits out his mouthful of martini. "Make magic public?"

Rook steps in, placing a hand on my shoulder once again. I watch with a smile as his bright-pink aura washes over me. "I know it's scary, especially to those of you who have been through the worst. But that's been my goal with the black market all along."

"You are responsible for the sale of Djinn blood?" Taj asks, standing so that his glass disappears. My heart races, and I stand as well, blocking Rook.

"It was my own blood," Rook admits.

"He's saved lives with it," I say. I don't want to mention it was him that sold the blood to Achan, reasoning that Alice was right and if Sophie was the result, then perhaps even evil can breed good things.

"No more," Taj says with finality.

"With all due respect, that's not your decision." Rook tightens his hand on my shoulder, and his aura shifts to red.

"It became my decision when it endangered those I love." Taj's eyes glow green with menace.

I will not have the two people I love most in this world hurt each other, so I intervene.

"We need to work together from here on out, not tear each other apart. We all want the same thing: peace and the chance to live our lives by making our own choices." The last is a reminder for Taj about what it's like to be forced to comply.

Taj's eyes dim until they are their normal shade of emerald, and Rook's aura fades back to pink.

"That's better," I say, sitting back down on the arm of the sofa. "If it wasn't impossible, I'd say what we need is a central governing body. Preferably one that's not corrupt." I snort at my own joke, having been privy to forcing political change worldwide behind the scenes for Kitra.

"That's brilliant," Rook and Taj say at the same time.

My jaw drops as I look between their earnest expressions. "That would be ridiculously hard to accomplish."

"But not impossible," Taj says, the corner of his mouth tilting upward. "We need to put out a call to all Djinn, hybrids, and magicians. Thanks to dear old Kitra, there are enough of us to not just call, but manage the meeting."

"I can help," Rook adds, eagerly caught up in whatever energy has invaded Taj. "We can use the club as a central meeting spot and enchant my tech to reach out to those who don't want to come in person. They'll get the info whether they like it or not!"

They continue excitedly making plans as the words meld together in my mind, becoming nothing more than gibberish and finally a low, constant buzzing. I think this is panic, but I'm not sure. I've never felt this before. It's like I'm floating, and I can't feel my body anymore. What just happened? I'd spoken up in the hopes of avoiding an altercation between them, and somehow, they'd begun making plans to alter the course of history. Everything could go wrong. One small slip, one magician or Djinni with bad intentions, could rain chaos onto everyone I love. Can't they see the danger here?

"Mira, Mira!" Taj's voice breaks through the buzzing, and I'm pulled back into the reality of the moment. My heart races, and I'm glad to find I'm seated because I'm afraid I'd be too dizzy to stand.

"I'm sorry, what?" I manage to say as Rook sits beside me and slides a comforting arm around me.

"This was your brainchild," Taj says, smiling wider than I've seen since he reunited with Caldor. "What part of this do you want? I think it may actually work."

"I don't...I think...you're both insane!" I stand and nearly fall onto Rook's lap as the world spins. "Do you know how dangerous it will be? We may be starting a war."

"Or ending one that's been going on for far too long," Taj says. His gaze meets mine, and I see the shadow of the past lingering there, inside, where we've all tucked it safely away.

My heart sinks to my stomach, and I'm once again grounded and in control. My whole long life I've been guided by fear. Fear of punishment, fear of retribution, fear of being a monster, fear of losing those I love. The only time I've found peace is when I am actively fighting against those that bring me that fear, whether through actual physical means or through stealing moments of love and light despite the imminent threat.

I sit back on Rook's lap, purposely close my eyes, and inhale his scent. Memories of making love to him, of his innocence, of his and Pops's choices to help others flood through me, and I know what I want —what I need to do.

The fear stops now.

"I'll run security," I say, and Rook tightens his hands around my torso. "You're better with words, Taj, and you're also the leader of the Order. You are the public face of this meeting. Rook, you run the tech and magic. I'll make sure no one interferes. We're going to give Leela and her baby a safer world or die trying."

"Nobody is going to die," Taj says, conjuring a new drink for all of us and raising a toast. "Here's to a better future."

"Hear, hear!" I agree, clinking glasses with Rook.

I may not share Taj's optimism, but I know one thing that settles my pulse and clears my head: What matters is the now and doing everything I can to protect it.

30

WEDDING PLANS AND BABY SHOWERS

THE PLANS FOR THE MEETING TAKE OVER ROOK'S AND TAJ'S LIVES, leaving little else they want to discuss or focus on. At least they grow closer as they plan. Taj enlisted the rest of the Order almost immediately, word spreading like lightning through those who'd been ready to close the veil. Dira jumped onboard with renewed vigor, and I don't have the heart to call her out on using it as an avoidance tactic. If it helps her deal with her grief for Ray, then what's the harm? That's how it was for me when I started with the Order. Avoid emotions at all costs. Until I realized that it's about living in those moments instead. I have to remember that her loss is far fresher than mine.

Leela and Jered are on board as well, but instead of helping plan the meeting, they've decided to get hitched beforehand, and all Leela's planning has gone into the upcoming nuptials. To my chagrin, she's asked me to be maid of honor, something I cannot say no to, though I detest the idea wholeheartedly, both for the traditional feminine role and for the gaudy entrapments. If I ever get married, it will be small, wild, and somewhere private. Just my loved ones and me. Not that I plan on any such thing. It's just that being dragged along with Leela as she shops and chooses various unnecessary frills forces such thoughts to the forefront of my mind.

"I don't know," Leela says, frowning at the cluster of fresh flowers before her. "I'm thinking lilies might be better suited to the venue. What do you think?"

After a moment, I realize that she's asking my opinion. In truth, my opinion is that neither lilies nor roses are necessary unless they grow naturally inside the walls of Chicago's illustrious Drake Hotel, where she's decided to have the ceremony and reception. She used magic to make room on their calendar, which I chastised, but instead of leaving the other couple high and dry, she found out the bride's first choice was a destination wedding in a castle in Ireland and gifted her with the money to make it happen.

"Why not just use magic and have the walls covered in vines with all manner of flowers?" I say, hoping to subtly point out that none of these human vendors are even necessary.

She cocks her head to the side, her bangs flopping into her eyes. "I suppose we could ask the florist to tastefully tack vines of pale-pink roses to the walls and then use lilies and orchids for the centerpieces. That would go with the color scheme."

For a moment, I thought I'd gotten through.

"How is the dress search coming?" she asks, biting her lip mischievously.

I pluck a fallen petal from the table and rub the soft material between my fingers. "To be honest, I haven't looked. I don't know why you want me to pick it out. You know I don't like frilly dresses, so I assumed you'll pick and I'll wear it."

Leela's hand covers mine, and I pause my assault on the delicate petal. She waits until I meet her gaze. She truly does glow with the child inside her. The golden aura may be the child's, but I wonder if it isn't also the magic of motherhood.

"Let's go to the next appointment then. I think we can do this together. And by the way, I never once used the word frilly."

I laugh at how her nose crinkles with the word and follow her outside the shop, promising she will make a decision soon and let the lanky woman behind the counter know what to prepare for the I.

Once on the sidewalk, she grabs my hand and backs us into the side of the building away from the window and the eyes of those brave enough to face the cold weather. She tugs me along as she transports us to New York, where we materialize before one of the many towering skyscrapers. Our breath fogs out in front of us as I crane my neck back to take in the surroundings. We're at another bridal salon, I realize, and from the opulent entrance she drags me through, I gather it's about as high class as it gets. At least it isn't Paris this time, as it always irritates me to be so close yet unable to drop in on Alice and Devon.

Leela chats with the receptionist, who offers us beverages while we wait, and I find we are soon seated on the pink velvet couch with champagne glasses filled with nonalcoholic bubbly. I sit, stiff-backed, wondering how long this appointment will take or whether she actually wants to find a dress or just play dress-up as Leela suddenly giggles uncontrollably.

"Are you all right?" I ask, setting down my glass.

"Oh, Mira! I felt him move." Her eyes shine like actual emeralds as she looks at me wide-eyed, grasping my hand and holding her stomach at the same time. She's never looked as beautiful as this moment, and it takes my breath away.

That is when a gentleman appears to welcome us.

"Which one of you is the bride to be?" he asks, gaze homing in on me.

"Her," I say quickly. "Leela here is the bride."

"Pleased to meet you," she says, standing with a hand over her stomach. "I have a feeling this is going to be my lucky day."

An hour later, and I wait alone on another velvet sofa in front of a dais surrounded by mirrors, white fluff, and repetitive *oohs* and *ahhs*. I've taken the liberty of switching to actual champagne that refills itself, and I sip at it, bouncing my leg.

My nose is buried in the fizzing drink when she finally makes her dramatic appearance, accompanied by the beaming gentleman at her elbow. She literally glows with a golden-and-silver sheen that envelopes her entire visage. The gown is simple compared to what she's tried on before, ivory silk that flows regally over her curves and ends in a short but elegant train. The sleeves are bell shaped, and the empire waist allows plenty of room for her growing bump. Tiny pearls line the edges of the waist and bodice where the tops of her breasts peek out. It's breathtaking.

She steps up onto the dais, facing away from me as the salesman adjusts the train perfectly and places a simple yet long veil on top of her head with a tiara. She beams at her own image, and I catch a glimpse of my own expression, mouth ajar and eyes protruding. I nearly laugh at myself, but I don't want her to mistake it for amusement at her appearance. If she's finally happy, I'm thrilled.

"So what do you think?" he asks, clasping his hands together with a smile.

"I love it!" Leela exclaims, turning to face me. "Mira?"

"It's perfect," I say, standing and setting aside my glass.

"Now for my maid of honor here," Leela says, clapping her hands together in glee.

I pick my glass up and let the salesman lead the way.

Three hours later, I'm exhausted and far from glowing. I would've been fine with the first dress they picked out, but after about twenty or more, I lost count at some point as my head grew dizzy from my bottomless cup. I am desperate for her to approve of something. I'm resigned to looking like a clown anyway.

"Hmm," Leela says, hand on chin as I twirl for her. "Not it."

I wave a hand, and the dress hangs itself back up. Before I can pull the next one off the hanger, a hideous pink chiffon, the salesman knocks on the door. "I have something I think you'll like."

I pull on a robe and open the door to the dressing room, eyeing the not-so-offensive material slung over his arm. When he hangs it up, I wonder if I'm finally drunk enough to actually like something.

It's a silk jumpsuit, with spaghetti straps, a plunging neckline, and wide legs. The color is a pale gold, and I have to admit would suit me quite well. I look up into the man's eyes, grateful and wondering if he has some form of magic himself that would explain how he figured out what I would want without me even knowing the information.

I pull it on, and it fits like it's made for me. I even spin in it, making Leela giggle uproariously.

"But it isn't orchid or pale pink," I say, knowing she's set on those colors.

"No, but it's perfect and will look lovely with a pink and orchid bouquet. We'll take it."

When we exit the building, it's dark outside, and the lights of New York glitter along the icy streets, the wind sweeping some of my tiredness away.

"What a wonderful day. Thank you, Mira." Leela tackles me with a hug so suddenly that I stumble, and we both nearly fall to the ground.

I hug her back, burying my head in the faux fur collar at her neck.

"Don't forget we have a date for Saturday!" she says, letting go and skipping backward a few steps like a sprite.

I groan. "But you found the dress."

"We have to go baby shopping, silly. I'll text you. It's time to go home and tell Jered everything."

I smile, shaking my head slightly as she disappears from the sidewalk. Stuffing my hands in my coat pockets, I turn and begin walking down Fifth Avenue, still crowded with pedestrians. New York is a good place to get lost in a crowd, and that sounds heavenly at the moment.

Ten minutes is all I get before my phone buzzes incessantly in my pocket. I've been lectured enough lately about paying attention to the damn thing that I pull it out with a grumble and put it to my ear.

"We have a problem," Taj says by way of greeting.

Fuck.

"What?" I ask as an explosion from somewhere nearby nearly knocks me off my feet. Chaos erupts all around me as the previously self-occupied crowds burst into shrieks, running in all directions. I hug the wall of the nearest building as Taj's voice continues in my ear.

"There's a rogue Djinni wreaking havoc on New York City."

31

IN THE BEGINNING

I CANNOT AVOID JUDE WHEN HIS MASTER IS CONSTANTLY IN AMAYA'S SHADOW.
It's as though he's become her puppy dog, and after altering his body for him,
he reminds me far too much of Achan and Cephas, lurking behind Kitra with
a mixture of hunger and fear in their eyes. Having fallen into this relationship
with Jude, those old days haunt me with a stronger presence than I've become
accustomed to.

Jude catches me in the hallway as he returns from fetching his master's
wife. I am on my way to retrieve the same man I was forced to torture in
front of him. He grabs my arm to stop me and sends the woman on her way
inside.

"You cannot avoid me forever. Whatever it is you're afraid of, I don't care.
I care about you, Mira. You've made my life worth something."

My chest squeezes, and I find it hard to draw in a breath.

"I am not good for you, Jude. This cannot last. Eventually we will be sepa-
rated, even if you can forgive me for what I've done. What I am forced to do."

He takes my face in his calloused hands and brushes the skin of my fore-
head with his thumbs. Tingles travel through my body, and I press my eyes
closed, afraid to move.

"If I have only one more moment with you, I choose that over a hundred
years as a free man."

*My eyes open, and the earnestness in his expression robs me of words.
Instead, I respond as he lowers his mouth to mine. The stolen moment is brief
but warms my heart, so frozen by terror. I smile at him as he continues into
the throne room, and I continue on to retrieve Ahmed.*

*When I appear with the doomed man before Amaya's throne, a hush falls
over the vast marble room. She steps lazily down from her perch on high to
face the example before her.*

*"How the mighty have fallen," she says, grasping his face so hard it is sure
to leave a bruise. The man is naked for humiliation's sake, as well as half-
starved and dehydrated from his stay in the dungeon.*

*"I've sworn my allegiance. What more do you want?" His voice is raspy
from disuse.*

I wait obediently beside him, expressionless and facing my master.

*"You are to be given a great honor, Ahmed," Amaya says, addressing the
room, filled with all the tribal heads she wishes to make an impression on.
"You will serve as a demonstration for your equals of the power under my
control, so that there will never again be a question as to who is in charge."*

*Ahmed shifts uncomfortably beneath her grasp, and I see the fear in his
eyes. His arms and fingers are better, but still bent at odd angles, having not
been set correctly after breaking. He doesn't dare raise a hand, not that he
could if he desired it.*

*"When you go back to your homeland," Amaya announces to the crowd,
her voice echoing around the space, "you may be tempted to be lax in your
faithfulness to me. But know that neither time nor space can hide your deeds
from my all-seeing eye. Isn't that right, Mira?" she asks, cold dark gaze
settling on me.*

*"Yes, Master," I respond immediately, a chill running along my flesh.
Why has she singled me out? I fight the urge to glance at Jude for fear of
giving anything away.*

Her thin lips curl into a smile. I know that smile—it is one of blood lust.

"I believe Ahmed will make a fine addition to my collection. Mira?"

*I raise my hands, willing my eyes to glow again for show as Ahmed
cowers, arms useless at his sides. In moments, he is encased in stone. He is the
thirty-fourth living statue I've crafted at my master's command. If I do not
keep count, who will?*

Murmurs rise all along the throne room as I stand back so they can witness what has happened. I relax internally when I see Amaya is pleased with the response.

"Place him outside the garderobe so he can forever watch the other filth of the castle."

I wave an arm, and it is done. A humiliation he will at least not be aware of.

"Excellent! Now to a vote. One at a time, each tribal head will approach me, kneel, and swear fidelity. If I or my Djinni sense any dishonesty or ill intent, you will join your friend."

One by one, starting with Jude's master who's already sworn a blood oath, they kneel, trembling before Amaya, and pledge their lives and their tribes' lives to her. When it is done, she declares it is time for celebration and grants each of them a wish, approved by her, which I am expected to grant.

I fill treasuries with gold and jewels, change appearances, and heal diseases for the already wealthy men. My wish would be to grant freedom for all their slaves, wives included.

The last man stands on the dais, head bowed. I am looking forward to slipping away, perhaps finding time for a tryst with Jude when he makes his wish.

"I wish for the company of this creature for the evening," he says, gesturing toward me.

It is unexpected, and my eyes widen as I search for Amaya's reaction. It is too late. She's seen the fear in my face even if only for a moment.

"Take her and do what you will so long as she's returned unharmed by morning." She waves me away, knowing full well that she has the power to call me back at any time if she needs me. I will not be that lucky, I'm sure.

I glance at the man as he grabs my wrist and hauls me off the dais. His eyes are small and set close together. He has a large mole on his cheek, and he is big enough to bring me physical harm since I cannot fight back without repercussions. I know better than to risk my master's wrath.

Still, I resign myself to being in his company until tomorrow, tuning out and paying little heed as he pulls me onto his lap, his erection already poking my thigh. With any luck, he will fall asleep and it will be over with quickly.

Without a word, he grasps the back of my head and pulls my face roughly to his, probing my mouth with his tongue. He squeezes my breast with his other hand, twisting painfully.

I don't see or hear Jude enter, so I am surprised when I am tugged off the man's lap and do nothing to prevent it when Jude shoves a dagger into his forehead.

"What have you done?" I shriek, hurrying to close the door.

Jude stands over the body, chest heaving and face ruddy with a rush of blood.

"I couldn't just sit back and watch another man take you against your will, not again. It's been destroying me inside that I allowed my own master to do so. I can't allow it again."

I tug on his arm. "Jude, I've been used many times and will be again. I am a slave, just as you. But what I can't bear is watching you pay the price." I begin to pace. "I will clean the spatter from you and send you back to your proper place. I can make this look like an accident, I think. Or I will tell her he wished for me to stab her with the dagger... Yes, she will not be pleased that I reacted in such a way, but it will be forgiven after a beating."

"Mira." Jude pulls me into his arms and shakes me lightly to get my attention. His face is still red, but his eyes are earnest as he searches my face. "Let's run away. We can go far away from here where they'll never find us."

"Oh, Jude," I repeat, shaking my head as tears spill hot and heavy down my cheeks. "I cannot run. She will simply call me back. I cannot break the magic hold she has over me. Nothing can break that." I place a hand over his heart. "I love that you would do this for me, but I can't allow it. I won't see you hurt because of me."

"I will hide you. I'll take you to every shaman in Africa until we break the spell. Mira, come with me. I need you." His grip on my arms is like the yoke on a mare.

"You are asking for something I cannot give, though I want to." I take his hand and place it over the choker on my neck. "Not as long as she has the matching stone."

"I see," Jude says, swallowing and looking away. But I'm not sure he does.

"I can make you forget me," I offer. It would take away his pain.

"No." He steps away, out of my grasp. "I don't ever want to forget you,

Mira. You are worth any pain. You are worth fighting for. It's going to be okay, Mira." He nods toward the body behind me and exits the room.

I glance at the lifeless man behind me, wishing not for the first time that I could bring the dead back to life.

32

HELLO WORLD, MAGIC EXISTS

"ALREADY ON IT." I SHOVE MY PHONE IN MY JACKET POCKET AND GO invisible before rising straight up into the night sky for a better vantage point.

Another earth-shattering explosion rocks the world as I land on the roof of the building housing the bridal salon. Thankful Leela already left, I narrow my eyes and scan the chaos below, searching for a sign of the source.

He's hard to miss, being that he's about forty feet tall. My gaze falls on his neck, searching for the type of stone he wears so that I can find his master and destroy the twin. My mouth falls open at the sight of bare skin around his throat. My gaze darts to his wrists as he grabs the top half of a brick skyscraper and crumbles it between his hands.

No bracelet either.

I'm more stunned by him choosing to wreak havoc while free than I am about his show-stopping manner. But I shake my head, clearing it before anyone else gets hurt, and take to the sky once again.

Time slows, and I throw out my own power to reinforce the structure he's trying to topple. I thrust my hands outward and apart as invisible forces pry his grip loose. He stumbles backward, nearly falling on another building as people rush around his enormous feet and cars honk from the streets at a standstill.

He's dressed in an outfit that belongs back in Kitra's island compound. His bare chest peeks out from beneath an embroidered gold vest, and the material of his pants billows out as he regains his balance. His dark hair flops in his face, and his glowing green eyes are as big as buses.

"Stop." I boom my voice out so it surrounds him, and he swats at me as I fly around his head. He can't see me, but he can feel me brushing by his hair like an insect. "You are endangering both humans and Djinn. Return to normal size immediately, or you will be dealt with."

He laughs, swiping out an arm. I dodge the blow, but the building I managed to save a minute ago isn't so lucky. The side crumples inward, glass shattering and rubble raining down on the streets below.

"That's it," I say. I shield myself and throw my power outward, wrapping him in a net of lead.

He fights the stinging sensation of his bonds, thrashing wildly as I rise into the sky as fast as possible to pull him out of reach of any more destruction. His tolerance for lead has not been developed as I'd assumed since he rapidly shrinks back to normal size, slipping easily through a hole. He must be relatively new to this world, I realize as I push him backward toward the water and the Statue of Liberty, hoping to avoid more devastation in Manhattan. The crisscrossed burns from the lead fade even as we fly forward through the air.

"I don't want to hurt you," I say, turning visible.

"Then why did you stop me?" he asks, slowing in midair and waiting for me to come closer.

I approach cautiously but notice with some relief that Dira and Taj appear behind him by several yards.

"What you were doing was reckless," I say. "You are endangering our own kind by demonstrating that we are a threat to humanity."

"We are a threat."

I snap my mouth shut and consider my next move. I'm not a diplomat like Taj. I don't have fancy words to persuade or talk people down. All I have is truth.

He takes my silence as encouragement.

"Why bother trying to placate them? They are lesser beings. I came here to fix what no one else has. They've hurt and enslaved our kind. It's time to show them real power."

"They aren't all bad," I say, but it sounds weak to my own ears.

He laughs. "What? Are you smitten with one or something? Come on. Help me do this, and we can save yours as a slave for our kind."

The thought of Rook as a slave stokes a fire inside me that burns so sudden and violently that I'm surprised I don't combust. I take it my face reflects my rage since the Djinni before me backs up a few yards, his smile melting from his face.

"No. More. Slaves." I enunciate each word so there can be no mistake. "No more pain. No more torture."

Taj glides between us along with Dira. "What is your name?" he asks the rogue.

"I will take no human name," he says, sneering. "And I'm tired of all this talking. We are Djinn, not human. Now get out of my way, or I will move you."

"You cannot. We outnumber you," Dira says matter-of-factly.

"Except that you spend too much time talking and not enough acting." The rogue's hands flick forward. I have just enough time to throw up a shield around myself, but not enough to protect Taj and Dira, who are encased in lead nets much like the ones I put him in.

The fire inside me blazes into an inferno, knowing the pain of the lead is cumulative and how much worse it is for them, especially Taj.

The *rogue's* mistake is cockiness and making the assumption that I will not strike.

Before he can process that I've avoided his trap, he's blown backward by a tornado of blue flame. I encase him in a box of lead, this time with no gaps to escape through and little room to move without brushing the sides.

I free my friends and spit at the box. "Fuck you."

Taj raises an eyebrow as he leans on Dira's shoulder, still floating in the air. "Thank you?"

I laugh. "You're welcome. Now get that out of my sight before I crush it with him inside."

Taj exchanges some sort of look with Dira before leaving with the box, murmuring, "What to do with you?"

Dira floats my way, one eyebrow cocked in question. "You okay?"

I shrug. "I'm fine. But I don't even know how to begin with damage control back there." I gesture toward the now distant cacophony of sirens and screams still ravaging Fifth Avenue.

She pulls my hand into hers and squeezes. "I don't know that we can. I mean, we can do a blanket spell that makes them forget, but surely there are already others that have left the scene or, knowing humans, shared the drama on the Internet. This on top of what happened at the Vatican is sure to be too much."

I nod, staring at the flashing lights and chaos with a lump in my throat.

Somehow, I don't think Rook's vision of a slow, controlled leaking of information is an option anymore.

33

FORCED DECISIONS

In hindsight, pacing the carpet in Rook's apartment was not the best decision, but since I did not trust myself to take part in the meeting below without succumbing to my temper, and with the tech in the bedroom set up to alert me to any mischief, I hadn't really considered alternatives.

"Did you think it would take them a few minutes to decide the fate of world?" I mutter to myself, followed by a dry laugh.

I conjure myself a glass of water and force my body to sit on the arm of the sofa to drink. Out the door and one flight below me are a collection of forty Djinn and magicians. Those who heeded the call and felt compelled to add their voice to the final outcome. The others signed magical contracts drawn up by Dira overnight that bind them at their word to abide by the decisions made so long as it didn't cause them or their loved ones harm.

Personally, no binding contract will ever sit right, whether it uses blood or not, but I understood the reasoning, so I let it go with the last caveat included. No matter what, the thought of so many powerful beings in a populated area has me on edge. Literally on the sofa edge, I suppose.

With a sigh, I send my empty glass to the sink and begin pacing again. It doesn't feel right just sitting here while everyone decides our fate. I trust Rook and Taj, and even Leela, but what of the others? Maybe I should have gone...

I review once again in my mind the backlash that the rogue unleashed less than forty-eight hours ago. By the time I reached Rook, he'd seen the news reports of the giant that attacked Manhattan. We'd held onto each other through the night, watching the news with the rest of the human world as journalists debated whether aliens or government experimentation was a more likely culprit. Thousands across the world panicked, taking or endangering others' lives in the certainty that it was the prophesized end times. By the time midnight rolled around, Rook had taken a call from Taj in his bedroom, and within an hour, he was back on the couch with a smirk on his face.

"What did you do?" I asked.

"Watch." Rook gestured to the television where Taj's face appeared, interrupting the footage I'd seen a hundred times of the rogue Djinni knocking the top of a building down onto the crowds below.

"Don't try to adjust your television. This is being broadcast on all devices across all languages," Taj said. "My name is Taj, and I am Djinn. I'm here to bring you answers about what happened tonight. My kind has existed in the shadows for thousands of years. You've heard of us in popular culture and storybooks. You've been taught to fear us, and I'm sorry to say that jerk who attacked New York fed into that. But the truth is we don't want to hurt anyone. We just want to live in peace. We've been hunted by humans for far too long but didn't want to come out publicly because of fear. I guess the one thing he did was force us to get over it. So here we are. We use what you call magic. There are other types of magical beings as well, including humans with powers. The individual who attacked earlier was an anomaly. I guess even humans have serial killers and school shooters. Anyway, he's been detained by us and is no longer a threat. I just wanted you all to know that we aren't bringing the end of the world or a great war or anything like that."

The TV flashed, sizzled, and the footage resumed. I remained speechless as Rook whooped his hands in the air and did a hip-swerving dance around the room. Soon the footage of buildings crushing innocent people was replaced by visions of Taj's face and more human debates.

And here we are, just over a day later, figuring out how to organize ourselves so that we can approach the leaders of humankind collectively.

As I reach for the door, unable to take another second of waiting, the knob twists, and it's thrown open to reveal Rook, his face flushed, his aura a dizzying swell of rotating color, and his lips pinched closed. I can't decide if he is elated or angry, and I'm about to shout at him to say something when he sweeps me up into his arms and answers me with a mind-blowing kiss that melts away all the anxiety I've built up over the past several hours.

I barely recall where I am as he releases me to slip down onto my own two feet. Then it all rushes back as he bursts into a mile-wide grin.

"I take it things went well," I say, unable to keep from matching his enthusiasm.

"Better than I could've imagined," he says, taking my hand and leading me over to the sofa as the door softly shushes shut.

"Tell me."

"There is a new magical governing board. It's got elected positions that rotate every four years, sort of like the American system. Taj refused to call it a council, so we're dubbing it the OEM, Order of Elected Magic. Of course, he's the president. Dira is vice-president. They wanted to nominate you, but we respected your decision to stay out of politics."

I narrow my eyes, recognizing the glint in his. "Do I detect a 'but'?"

He laughs, a deep and musical sound that makes it difficult to stay suspicious. "You've been appointed a very special position."

Before I register what's happening, I stand and open my mouth to argue. Rook holds up a hand to stop my tirade before it starts.

"Don't worry. It's something I think you'll like, and if not, you can respectfully decline."

I cock my hip and fold my arms. "Go on."

"Really, there are two positions that would fall under the heading of security. One is what we're calling the Monitor, and the other is the Enforcer. I'm the Monitor."

Understanding dawns, and I relax my stance. "Then we'd be working together?"

Rook nods, watching me carefully for a reaction.

"Enforcer." I roll the word around, liking the feel of it. "Yeah, that's kind of badass."

"The way you handled the rogue the other night, well, that took some quick thinking and skill. You really found a balance between physical force, mental acuity, and kindness. If you don't mind my saying so, Mira, the story was pretty hot. I wish I'd been there."

I smile as he pulls me down to the couch with him, and I straddle his lap, letting my hair shield our faces. "I don't ever mind you saying I'm hot."

I brush my lips against his in a tease as we nuzzle our noses together. I slide my palm down the center of his chest, but he sets a hand on mine, halting me.

"One more thing first."

I groan, letting my hand slip to the waistband of jeans so that I can at least enjoy his ragged breathing as he continues talking.

"I thought you should know that Leela and Jered have important roles too. They'll be the public faces of the magical community. They're perfect, a family unit representing Djinn, magician, and hybrid."

I sit up straight. "Isn't that dangerous? What if some whack job thinks they're spawn of the devil or some shit and goes after them?"

Rook takes my face in his hands. "Then it's even more important that we do our jobs to protect them. I'm going to start setting up the equipment first thing tomorrow so that we'll be alerted the second something happens. Don't worry, babe. Your sister knows the risks, and we're going to keep them safe."

I nod and allow him to finally pull me in for the deep kiss I'd been hoping for. But even as my body responds in kind, my mind buzzes with the information he's just given me. The whole world has changed in what feels like a moment, and Rook is excited about it.

"You're worried," he says, reading my thoughts, probably literally. He strokes my hair and searches with empty amber eyes.

"I don't understand how you aren't," I admit.

"Of course I am. But my hope is stronger than my doubt."

I lean into the space between his shoulder and neck, inhaling his scent. "I was a slave for over a thousand years."

He rubs my back, slowly drawing his hands up and down my spine as I try to get the words out.

"I lost hope many times over. The hardest part was gaining it back for a brief but beautiful heartbeat. It was so difficult because the part that came after pulled me further down like a riptide each time. So when I ride that wave, high above into the swell, I know all too well what waits for me in the dark depths below."

"Mira." Rook takes my upper arms and pushes me upright so I can see his face. "You keep riding the waves anyway, and that's what makes you so amazing."

I harrumph but keep listening.

"You've been through things I can't even imagine. The scariest of situations. But you are the one who ultimately came out on top."

"What if that's only true at the moment?" I ask, pressing my forehead to his. "What if I crash and burn worse than ever?"

"You're mixing metaphors again," he teases.

I roll my eyes. "You know what I mean."

"Look, I can't guarantee anything about the future. You know that, and I'm not going to pretend it'll all be okay. But I can tell you that living each day like we're on top and loving freely, well, that's where happiness lives. In the moment."

"In the moment," I agree, leaning in once again to meet his lips. This time the kiss continues as I slide against him, feeling him grow beneath his clothes and enticingly near my center.

We tear at each other's shirts and pants until we are bare, and he guides me down to the couch where he takes each nipple in his mouth and rotates his tongue around them until they stand erect and I squirm against him, needing more. Happy to comply, he works his mouth down over my stomach, gripping my hips firmly to hold me steady as he explores the heat between my legs, dipping his tongue into the folds of flesh and working it over the swollen nub that's crying for attention.

"Take me," I command.

He guides me to my knees, facing the back of the sofa and enters me from behind, rough, hard, and all at once. I growl with intense and overwhelming sensation as he fills me fully and then pulls out maddeningly slowly before filling me again.

"You're going to torture me?" I ask, gripping the cushions before me.

In response, he places one hand over my breast and one over my clit as he begins driving inside me faster and faster, bringing me to the edge and then spilling over again and again until he too is spent and we remain a quivering mass of flesh on the couch.

"You're incredible," he says over my mouth.

"Ditto." I cup his butt in my hand and squeeze, teasing him into another round.

We may have a busy day tomorrow, but right now I plan to ride the crest of this wave all night long.

34

IN THE BEGINNING

THE MORNING DAWNS BRIGHT, THE OCEAN UNUSUALLY CALM BELOW. I SIT ON the edge of my favorite spot where Jude and I first made love, wondering why life is so cruel. Even the weather mocks me. Perhaps they are right when they call me a devil in hushed voices. Maybe that's why I deserve this.

I waited for so many years for Kitra to meet the cruel end she deserved, only to feel her sting one last time as her daughter, as spoiled and cruel as her mother, took possession of the stone, letting me know that her mother died peacefully in her sleep. Sometimes I swear I see the same glint of malice in each of her descendants' eyes when they inherit me. Perhaps it is the power of the binding stone that causes the madness. After three masters, I decided it didn't matter where it came from—it simply was.

When I am summoned through space to my master's feet, I know what will happen, but this time it hurts more than ever, excepting perhaps the day this started. Seeing Rhada's empty body on the wall as Leela's fingers pressed the ruby to my neck...

I attempt to betray no emotion as I prostrate myself on the ground at her feet. "You've called, Master."

"Stand, slave." I know by the way she names me that she means to punish me no matter what the cause.

I comply.

"Why have you killed the man who took you last night?"

One glance at the room shows me that Jude and his master are among those already present, watching and listening curiously. I try not to meet his eyes, but Jude is impossible to look away from, the headstrong and idiotic determination to do "right" clear on his face.

"I am sorry, Master. It was an accident. He enjoyed dangerous play." The lie slides easily off my tongue, but I doubt it will matter.

"Then why did you not come tell me right away? And why, Mira, would you have made such a mistake when you know what's at stake and have never done so before?" She leans forward, clear, cold eyes making me shuffle and twist my fingers.

"I was afraid." I shrug.

"As you should be." Amaya sits straight in her throne, conjuring lead shackles around my ankles and wrists that pull me to the ground with their weight. Immediately the pain like a thousand needles sinks into my skin, draining my energy and fogging my brain.

"Stop!" Jude steps forward, face deep red and muscled arms tensed.

I press my eyes closed, wishing I could prevent it.

"What have we here?" Amaya asks, sounding far too much like a cat with a mouse.

"It was I who killed the sheikh, not Mira." He is at the foot of the dais, sandaled feet beside me, yet out of reach.

"And why would you do such a thing?"

"Because this woman is not a toy. She deserves the freedom to choose her own partner."

Murmurs break out all around us, but it's like the buzzing of flies in my ears. It has only solidified his fate. A tear slips from the corner of my eye and down my cheek, sizzling onto the chains on my wrists.

"And why would you not tell the truth, dear Mira?" Calling me dear is even more dangerous than calling me slave.

I swallow back the words I want to utter. I can't admit it. It would be worse for him.

"The fool thinks he is in love with me. I did not anticipate foolishness

would be deserving of death in your eyes, Master." It is the best I can offer him.

I can't look at him. I know I've hurt him. But better hurt than dead.

"That isn't the sort of decision, nor even thinking that a slave of your position should be doing. We shall have to remedy that immediately lest you start thinking you are more than a trained animal here for my pleasure."

Jude's swift movement catches my eye, and I look up in time to see him leap onto the dais and reach for my master. She flicks her finger, and he is knocked off and onto the ground as she stands.

"You dare attack me?" she roars down at him even as he stands again, murder in his eyes.

"Please don't," I manage in a weak voice. I'm not sure if I'm pleading with him or her. It doesn't really matter. It won't help, but I have to try. This time I cannot sit idly by.

Jude hesitates, and Amaya laughs, pushing me to the marble floor with a slippered foot to my neck.

"It has feelings for the slave man." She snaps, and Jude struggles to lunge again, unable to move his legs from the spot where he stands. He reaches with arms and fists but finds only air. "Very well then, this is quite entertaining. Everyone, gather round, and we shall watch as my Djinni learns once and for all that she is not human and will never have what she desires."

I feel the crowd gather, the buzzing growing in my head as the effects of the lead grow stronger. What cruelty does she have in mind for us?

I don't have to wait long to find out as she releases me from my bonds and barks at me to stand and approach my lover.

"Do you want him one last time, Mira? Before you say good-bye?"

I do not answer. If I react, she will certainly force us to make love in front of everyone, and I do not want that humiliation for Jude.

"No, perhaps not. Perhaps he is not deserving of any further pleasure. Surely as a man, he would relish it." Amaya tightens her fist before her, and Jude becomes rigid, unable to move, save his eyes and mouth. I stand beside him, awaiting my fate.

"Do you suppose that my pet here would not dare to hurt you?" She coos, taking his face in her hand, digging her nails painfully into his flesh.

He spits at her, and her eyes flash dangerously. My heart sinks.

"Break his hands, Mira."

I cannot avoid the sharp intake of breath as I move to complete my command. I do it quickly, unable to meet his eyes.

"I forgive you, Mira," he whispers. "I know you feel you have no choice."

I dart my own angry gaze at him in response. It is far more than a feeling. If I could in any way fight this, I would do so.

"Now his arms," Amaya says, circling us within the outer ring of onlookers.

Soon he is a broken mess on the floor, crying in pain, and my heart is there along with him. I send him as much silent healing as I dare.

"Now heal him," Amaya says, a smile lighting her face.

My shock must show, but I immediately comply, helping him to his feet.

"Good. Now do it again."

She turns away and steps back up and onto her throne as I begin the torture over again, knowing this may last far too long.

Indeed it is after several rounds of bringing my lover to near death, and beyond begging for it, that she finally stops the madness.

"Heal him and stop," she commands.

Jude's skin is as white as chalk, a sheen of sweat covers him head to toe. I want to scream and cry, but I cannot. What good would it do but nudge her on?

"Do you see she is a monster yet?" Amaya asks.

Jude's unfocused eyes wobble as he turns slowly toward me. "You are the monster, not she."

Before she can command worse, I shoot a bolt of green lightning at him from my fingertips. His body jolts and trembles as he's lifted from the ground. When I can stand no more, I drop him, and he lands limp at my feet.

Amaya laughs. "As long as you know what you are, Mira, then I have succeeded." She leans back and crosses her long legs. "Let him stand when he can, and we will finish this."

I wait, watching as he struggles shakily to his feet. I do not reach to help. I am the reason he suffers. That much she is right about. But if I am a monster, she is a hundred times worse.

When he stands, hands fisted yet trembling, I refuse to meet his gaze.

"Mahmood, this is your slave. What say you to the fate I decide for him?"

Amaya asks. Her tone is considerate, but I know that she will do what she wants and asks only to be certain of his loyalty.

"Jude has been faithful to me since captured in war. I regret that this demon has affected his soul such. But whatever fate you decide, I shall find fair and just."

Amaya smiles. He's passed her test. "You will be rewarded with a new slave in his stead. Mira will find one for you that does the job just as well."

I nod and bow in acknowledgment.

"Look your lover in the eyes as you turn him to stone. And, Mira?"

"Yes, Master?"

"Do it slowly."

I do as commanded, which is all I am able. And I watch the emotions flicker across his face as his flesh gradually changes to unforgiving marble. Shock, fear, anger, hopelessness, and finally all I see is love as his pupils glint with the light of the sun overhead reflecting off the surface of the stone.

Broken. My insides are as broken as Jude was so many times this day at my own hand. This is what comes of hope. This is what comes of desire and selfishly taking anything for myself. How many times will I have to learn this lesson before the Mira inside me no longer exists?

"Good job, Mira. Send him to his proper place outside the throne room so you may visit him as often as you wish, and then dance for us."

35

VOWS

Leela is the most beautiful bride I've ever seen. It's more than the aesthetic she's somehow pulled off to perfection. It's the glow that literally surrounds her and Jered. The auras pulse over them in shades of lavender and gold, swirling and quite nearly dancing in a hypnotic way. They can't keep their hands or their gazes off each other the entire evening, and the bump beneath Leela's dress only makes her look more breathtaking.

Rook squeezes my hand beneath the table and leans to whisper in my ear, his breath washing over me and causing tingles all over my body. "The energy is beautiful. It makes me want to do this too."

I can't help the way my pulse races and my head dizzies in response to his words. I take a gulp of champagne, and at a complete loss for anything else, I stand, clinking the side of my glass.

"A toast to the happy couple!" The room quiets. "Leela, you and I haven't always seen things eye to eye. But I've always envied your ability to express yourself in so many ways, and your bravery."

Leela laughs lightly, and I clear away the lump growing in my throat. "You are my sister in every way that counts, and if anyone ever tried to hurt you, I would have their head mounted on my wall. Literally."

Laughter flows from the guests despite my seriousness. But I continue. "Jered has proved his worth, though, many times over. He's been there for all of us and is, well, part of the family. To family!" I raise my glass in the air, unable to continue without losing my cool, and the room erupts into a chorus of clinking glasses until the happy couple kisses for the hundredth time.

"Aren't you going to dance, Auntie Mira?"

I look over to find Sophie at my side, her honey-colored hair pulled up into a mass of curls. The outlandishly wide flower girl dress adorned with petals in the skirt somehow suits her. Her wide blue orbs appear innocent, but I still glare at Rook, suspicious.

"I didn't say a word. I promised I wouldn't force you," he says in response to my thoughts.

"The truth is, Taj promised to dance with me if I could get you two out there. Please? I really want to dance." She tugs at my arm as Rook rises from his seat.

I should have seen this subterfuge coming.

"I promise not to step on your toes," Rook whispers as he guides me forward with a palm on my back, Sophie still pulling my hand.

I roll my eyes and sigh, purposely trying to be melodramatic since I have to admit the thought isn't as bad as I'd anticipated. There's something about the energy in the room, the excitement and the music that combines to soften my resolve.

Being in Rook's arms, swaying among my family and friends, ignites a pilot light inside me. It's like a small glowing ember has been rekindled that was long ago snuffed out, and now, here, I feel safe enough to let it shine. No matter what happens, I will protect that tiny light with everything I have.

A tear slides down my cheek and onto Rook's tuxedo jacket. I hear him in my mind as clear as if he's whispering in my ear.

I think you are finally beginning to heal, Mira. I'm glad I can be a part of that.

I smile against his chest and lose myself in the song and the moment.

When the ballad ends and the fast music starts, I guide Rook to the sidelines and laugh as Taj and Cal take turns twirling Sophie until she's dizzy. It takes me by surprise when someone touches my arm, and I glance over to find the little girl's mother at my side.

"Hello, Elle," I say in greeting.

She smiles, but it's strained, and I'm instantly on alert. "May I have a word with you?"

I nod my consent and excuse myself to follow her outside in the cool night air beneath a smattering of stars above the city.

From here, the sounds of the reception are faded and distant to the point they feel more like a memory than something happening in real time. I hug myself and stare out at the scenery.

"What can I do for you?" I ask as she joins me at the edge of the railing to look out into the night.

Elle fiddles with the edges of her lacy sleeves. It takes a few minutes for her to speak, but I'm in no hurry.

"It's about magic," she finally says.

I raise my eyebrows but don't look at her. I simply wait for her to elaborate.

She sighs when I don't respond. "I admit I was a bit hysterical when I found out. And when I realized Leela, you, Taj, and Cal all had the same eyes, well, it sort of hit me hard."

It's my turn to sigh now.

"Then Corrie tells me that she's known all along and that not only Jered, but my own daughter are infected—"

"Excuse me?" I interrupt, facing her.

She shuffles, having the decency to at least look embarrassed. "I'm sorry, that was a bad choice of words. But you have to under-stand—this is all out of left field, and not only that, it's a secret you deliberately kept from me. One that involves my baby. One that's dangerous."

I draw in a deep breath, hoping for calm, but turn to look out at the stars in case my eyes glow. I don't want her to think I'm going to attack or infect her or anything. I grip the edge of the rail a bit too hard to ground myself.

"It was your husband who lied. He was the one to 'infect' your daughter and endanger all of you. He was also the one that started this as I'm sure you are now aware."

In my peripheral vision, Elle lowers her head. "Yes. I am aware. At least that's the story I've been told."

"Are you accusing me of something?" I ask point-blank. I don't have time or energy for anything other than truth at this moment.

"No!" She steps back, holding her hands up in fear. I simply continue to grip the banister and wait. "It's not that. It's just...the whole world feels upside down, and I couldn't very well ask Jered or Leela the hard questions. Sophie is too young and wouldn't understand. And Taj, well, to be perfectly honest he makes me nervous. I get the feeling he's put spells on me before or something."

She isn't wrong about Taj, but she is about Sophie. She'd be surprised what that child can handle.

"So you've come to me with your 'hard questions.'"

She nods hastily, and I wave a hand, conjuring a couple of cushioned seats for us as well as a lit firepit for warmth. I'm sure she must be chilly out here without a coat.

She jumps slightly but sits a moment after I do, folding her hands in her lap.

"How do I know you don't present a danger to my children?" she asks and then holds her breath. Her pale, trembling state softens me slightly.

I want to be angry and spiteful to this ignorant woman. But I also understand how brave she is being in the interest of protecting her children. I cannot fault her for that. What I have now is an opportunity, I realize. When humans feared me in centuries past, it was because of the manipulation of evil masters. I am a free Djinni now, and if I frighten this woman, it's because I choose that. And since the decision is my own, I know what I must do.

"I understand how scary this all can seem," I say, smiling and leaning forward. "It feels like deceit, and while I cannot excuse that, I can tell you that anything we may have done was only to protect you and your family from what you're going through right now."

The woman's shoulders relax slightly, and she offers a weak smile.

"I'm happy to answer any questions you have, and I think you'll find that Leela, Jered, and even Taj will as well. My brother may be a bit of a jokester, but he understands the gravity of this situation and wants peace more than anyone I know. You may even find that Sophie can have a deeper dialogue with you than you've given her credit for. She's quite the intelligent and talented child."

Elle sits up straighter in the chair, blinking away her surprise at my last statement. I conjure two cups of coffee and offer her one.

"I don't suppose it's spiked?" she asks with a laugh.

"I can arrange that." I tap her cup and smile as the top fills with a swirl of whipped cream. "Irish cream and coffee liquor."

"Thank you," she says and takes a sip. "I really appreciate you being so understanding. I know I'm probably blowing the conversation, but that's why I couldn't ask them." She nods toward the party inside.

"Well, I'd rather you ask than make assumptions." I sip on my own drink and cross my legs.

She nods and lets out a last stressful breath. "I think Corrie was getting a bit annoyed with me. And my other two children think it's the coolest thing ever. They keep asking Sophie to do tricks. Is that dangerous? I mean is there a cost to her using her magic?"

"Good question, Elle. No. If it is a very strong spell, then it can drain her energy, but she should recover. If it's something serious, I recommend asking one of us, but things like small tricks to entertain her siblings should be fine." I smile, proud of my composure when this conversation could have turned out very differently.

I wonder how many of these conversations are going on all over the world right now. How many times will we have to do interviews like this one in the public eye in order to calm the populace? I'm glad that's not my job. I don't envy Leela and Jered being our spokespeople.

"We should probably get back to the party," I say after a moment.

"One more thing," Elle says, stopping me with a hand on my wrist.

I settle back into my seat and nod.

"I know about Leela's history, and I guess your history too. Corrie explained it so she wouldn't have to. I'm sorry that happened to you.

You seem like such a nice woman, so together. I don't know how you do it."

I smile again, not trusting words at this point. What I'd like is for her to get to the point.

"Is there any danger of it happening again? I mean, what if someone takes control of you and you become, for lack of a better word, a weapon?"

I wave away the cups and the fire, standing. "Elle, I appreciate your concern, but if you are asking if there is still evil out there, the answer is undoubtedly yes. Will it win? I will do everything in my power to make sure that doesn't happen. But know that I swear I would never purposely hurt anyone who hasn't hurt my family first."

Elle's mouth drops open as I turn to walk away with a Cheshire cat grin. I have a party to get back to.

36

DAYBREAK

THE SUN SEEPS THROUGH THE BLINDS, PAINTING STRIPES OF LIGHT ACROSS the bed. I've been awake for at least an hour, propped on an elbow, watching the man beside me sleep. I've studied every groove and swell of his gorgeous chest as it rose up and down in a steady rhythm. His amber eyes are closed and rove back and forth beneath his lids as he wafts in and out of dream state, his long black lashes kissing the tops of his sculpted cheeks.

Lazily, I trace the line down the center of his stomach, edging back the sheets from his waist so I can see the way his waist angles down to his generous cock, swollen and ready for a morning romp. I'm so close to waking him with my mouth on it, but I'm also enjoying watching him more than I have a right to.

This is what normal looks like, and I revel in it.

The phone buzzes on Rook's other side, and he stirs. I hate those things.

Reaching over him, I stretch to retrieve it, and seeing that it's Taj's number, I silence it and set it back down. He can wait.

Rook cannot, however, as I seem to have woken him. And I find myself trapped over his lap, with his hand roaming down and over my ass to the sensitive area between my legs. The thoughts about what I planned to do with him have me wet and ready, and he lets a low rumble out of his throat as he presses forward, exploring with his fingers.

Before I know it, I'm on my back and his glorious body is aligned with mine, prodding at my entrance as he kisses me soundly.

"Good morning to you too," I say.

In answer, he pushes inside me, stealing my breath as he drives upward to my center.

"Mmmm," I murmur appreciatively as our hips move in unison. I grip his shoulders, urging him farther in.

He complies and rocks into me so hard that entire bed squeals in protest. My moans are louder than its complaints though, and when I reach my peak, Rook drives in hard, finding his own release.

The phone buzzes again, and Rook reaches over to pick it up, still inside me.

"Hello?" he says as he playfully pushes into me one last time.

"Finally, you pick up. Don't tell me Mira doesn't have her phone on again?" Taj's voice comes over speakerphone, and Rook rolls off me, replacing his cock with his unoccupied hand and lazily stroking me into a renewed frenzy.

I bite my lip to prevent myself from calling out.

"She's busy at the moment. What's up?" Rook says, circling my clit with his thumb and sliding two fingers inside me.

"I have a meeting with the president in an hour. I want my security team to make sure no one decides to take advantage of it by pulling anything."

"The president?" Rook repeats, hastening his pace on me until I pull a pillow over my own head to drown out my moans.

"I know. Not very much notice. But I decided not to be too picky about it at this stage. We've spoken over the phone, and the plan is to do a brief press conference and then speak in more detail privately."

"Hold on a sec." Rook puts the phone down as I peek from under the pillow, nearly mad with need. He slides another finger inside me and uses his other hand to press and rub on my clit until I cry out with my orgasm.

Rook rolls away again and picks up the discarded phone, taking it off mute. "Okay, we'll be at your place in half an hour. We have a few things to take care of here first."

"Tell Mira that's enough orgasms for one morning. You two can fuck again later. We have a job to do."

I sit up straight in the bed.

"I wouldn't mind another orgasm before your meeting," Cal's voice calls over the other line.

Rook and I laugh together as he hangs up.

"Lucky guess," I say, staring at the phone with suspicion.

An hour later, Taj and I enter the White House, ushered inside by secret service men in black suits and sunglasses with tech pieces in their ears.

"How very cliché," says Taj, winking at a particularly handsome one with raven curls at the door to the press room.

Of course we've dressed a tad cliché ourselves. I'm in a black leather bodysuit that affords me freedom of movement. Plus I like it. Taj is in a designer Armani with an emerald tie and matching handkerchief poking out of his breast pocket to "match his eyes."

There are a limited amount number of journalists invited to the event peppered across the room. Taj is shown to a podium set up beside the main one with an eagle spread across the front and a flag behind it. I stand behind him and to the side, imitating the stance of the secret service agents that surround the periphery.

They are of little consequence as none of them seem to have magician's auras and I spy no Djinn. But I do note a couple of brightly colored auras in the press seats. One in particular draws my eye as it cascades in shades of almost neon yellow and orange.

I narrow my eyes, trying to discern the emotions that may accompany this, and decide that the young woman it belongs to is terrified. I wonder if she fears us or is that nervous about the opportunity for such a large story.

The president is announced, breaking my concentration, and he strides in flanked by security to take his place at the podium next to Taj. I can't help but notice he is a few steps higher and therefore gives the illusion he is taller.

He and Taj exchange pleasantries. Taj presents him with a gift of a golden eagle that receives quite a few *oohs* and *ahhs* from the audience. Cameras flash and hands raise, eager to ask questions about magic and what the new policies will mean.

I continue to watch the woman with the neon aura as she directs the cameraman to get a better shot and then works her way around the room toward the other side of the stage, closest to Taj. Something about it doesn't sit right, but a magician should bear little danger if I remain alert.

She works her hand slyly into her pocket, and I feel the presence of lead before I see it. But when her gaze darts to her cameraman at the front of the room, snapping pictures of the president, understanding dawns.

Time slows as I throw out both my hands in either direction. One, melting the lead object into ash, and taking the woman's hand with it. The other yanks the camera from her accomplice's hands, causing it to fly across the room to me.

The president's bodyguards react immediately, covering him and pulling him from the room. The woman clutches her ruined hand, drops to her knees, and screams. The cameraman tries to run, but Taj catches on and yanks him back up on the stage with invisible hands.

I spot the magic on the camera instantly and crush the object in my hand.

"You were about to kill the president with magic," I say to the man struggling to run from the stage in vain.

Other cameras flash, and reporters thrust microphones toward us. The men in suits keep them at a distance.

"Tell the truth if you want to live," I state, glaring at the man, who's finally stopped trying to escape.

"She did it! Tracy has magic. She was going to slip some sort of ring on one of you and make you take the blame."

My vision turns scarlet, and I reach out to the woman sobbing on the ground until she floats into the air and onto the ground before me.

"Give me the ring and the matching stone," I say, barely controlling my fury.

She reaches for her pocket with her good hand and tosses out the ring and matching sapphire. I crush them with my boot.

The staff around us deal with dispersing the reporters and taking the woman and her cameraman away along with what's left of the evidence. They assure us she'll be treated medically, but frankly I couldn't care less.

"You saved the life of the president," the man Taj flirted with says to me, offering a hand. "The whole world is going to know you're a hero."

I take his offered hand when he persists and shake it.

"He'd like to see you both in his office," someone else says from Taj's other side.

It's the last thing I want to do right now, and thankfully Taj reads it on my face. "I've got this. You go ahead home. Good work though. And, Mira?"

I look at him, dazed.

"Thank you."

I pull my old friend into a hug. "We will always have each other's backs."

He squeezes me tighter in response. "Always."

I leave the grounds of the White House the human way, not wanting to offend, and then pop over to the club, where I promised to meet Rook when I was done.

The place is empty this early of course, except for the blue-haired bartender who's got the glasses cleaning themselves as she measures out different amounts of colorful liquids into a decanter on the bar.

"Well, hello there, Mira. Want to test out my latest concoction? I'm calling it a truth bomb."

I cross my arms and cock my head in question.

"Yeah, it makes it easier to tell the truth. I figure it'll be a good boost for shy folks. Also might make someone slip up if they try to roofie anyone. I can offer them if someone is sus."

"Good plan, Amy," I say, straddling a stool.

"They should taste like cherries though." She pours the final teal liquid into a small glass and slides it toward me.

I sniff it and then gulp. "It does taste like cherries."

She smiles, satisfied. "So? Tell me a truth. Let's see if it works."

I grin, ready to laugh, but instead words fly from my mouth when I open it. "I'm scared as hell now that magic's in the open."

She nods somberly.

I find myself continuing. "I love my life right now, more than I ever have before, and yes, I should live for each moment, but I have reason to be scared."

She leans forward over the bar and refills my glass while taking a swig of her own.

"I think it's okay to be scared as long as you don't let it control your life."

I take another sip and swirl the glass between my fingers, watching the glowing mixture cling to the sides of the glass. "There is something that's different this time around."

"What's that?" she asks.

"There are a whole hell of a lot of us that have learned to support each other. I guess you could say we've matured over the last millennium." I finish off the second round, enjoying the warm feeling swelling in my stomach.

She sits back and grins, gaze rising and focused behind me.

I turn to find Rook leaning on the railing at the top of the stairs in front of his apartment. I smile.

"It's a new day, and I believe things will be different this time."

I push off my stool and head for the curving steps so I can meet my love.

EPILOGUE

SIX MONTHS LATER

Holding a newborn makes me more nervous than chasing down the trio of Djinn I had to detain last week, but when the sweet bundle is in my arms, something inside me melts. In his soft blue blankets covered in lambs, little Gabriel blinks up at me, a tiny thumb shoved in his mouth.

"He's amazing," I say in complete and utter awe.

"We think so," Leela agrees, smiling at her husband, who stands behind her, his hand on her shoulder.

I study the tiny face as it studies me. His eyes are dark like his father's, and there's something in them that feels far too knowing for a tiny human. A blond curl falls onto his wrinkled forehead, and I brush it gently away.

Rook squeezes my shoulder, mirroring Jered. "My turn?"

"Not yet," I say, rocking my new nephew.

"We wanted to ask you both if you would consider being Gabe's godparents," Jered says.

I look over to them to see if they're serious, and Leela beams back at me, biting her lip in an expectant way.

"We'd be honored," I say, heart full to bursting. I stand and deliver the child to Rook, who seems far too natural holding him.

I study his face as he bounces the baby, and Leela chatters on about plans for enchanting his room with interactive mobiles and rocking horses.

Little Gabe cries out, sounding like one of the tiny sheep on his blanket, and Leela takes him gently from Rook to feed him.

Rook sits beside me and takes my hand in his, running his thumb along my knuckles.

They have a pretty beautiful life, he says in my head.

I nod.

Have you decided yet?

Rook surprised me about a week ago by kneeling on the ground and asking me to marry him. He'd waited until Taj and Cal's plans were well under way, but I still haven't given him an answer. I suppose I owe him one.

Only if it's a yes.

Dammit, I don't know if I'll ever get used to him reading my thoughts.

"If you'll excuse us, we have to be somewhere soon," Rook says, pulling me up, fingers still laced through mine.

Leela squeals a little and says good-bye.

It's like she knows something. *What exactly are these plans you speak of?*

"You'll see."

Rook tugs me into the air after him, and we fly through space, slowing time and appearing in Paris at the same café where we met Daffodil so long ago. There is a table set with candles and fairy lights on the patio with a rose in a vase at the center.

"Have a seat," Rook says, gesturing toward the setup.

I purse my lips but sit, and he pulls a bottle of champagne from an ice bucket to the side.

"A toast," he says after pouring two glasses.

I raise mine and tip the edge to his.

"To the love of my life."

We drink, and my insides grow warm, not entirely from the booze.

A waiter comes out and presents us with a platter of appetizers. I pop one in my mouth as Rook stands and comes around to once again kneel in front of me.

"Rook," I start.

"Mira," he says so loudly I wonder if the entirety of Paris can hear him. "Marry me."

"Rook."

"I made you something," he says and holds out a small box.

Oh no. It's a ring, isn't it?

He laughs and pops it open for me.

I stare for a moment, completely dumbfounded, and remove it from the box with trembling fingers. On the simple silver band are three round stones. On one side is a tiny opal. On the other is a tiny tiger's eye. In the center is a larger ruby. My pulse speeds up until it's hard to breathe.

"There are no matching stones," Rook assures me. "The only binding magic here is love. I want you to know that if you put this on, you own my heart forever, and that this is the way these things are supposed to work. You've told me what Kitra did, and I want you to know that for the rest of my life, I intend to do the opposite."

I run a finger over the stones, feeling for any magic, though I know none is there. Finally, I slip it on my ring finger, and all three stones morph into diamond hearts. I gasp.

"It changes depending on your preference," Rook says, still waiting on his knee.

Tears fill my eyes, and I throw my arms around his neck, sinking to the ground with him.

"Is this a yes?" Rook asks as we topple over.

"Yes. A thousand times, yes."

Thank you for reading! Did you enjoy? Please add your review because nothing helps an author more and encourages readers to take a chance on a book than a review.

And don't miss more from Lizzy Gayle with her sci-fi romance LOVE AT 20,000 LEAGUES. Turn the page for a sneak peek!

You can also sign up for the City Owl Press newsletter to receive notice of all book releases!

SNEAK PEEK OF LOVE AT 20,000 LEAGUES

I'd never felt so vulnerable. The ocean closed above me, swallowing the shuttle into a suffocating vastness that made me itch to claw at the 360-degree windows. Obviously, that would have been useless, but it was hard to turn away from the unending view. So, I hugged myself in an attempt to stifle my panicked urges and found a seat in the circular back-to-back rows of the luxury pod.

Not only were there thousands upon thousands of tons of water pressing in on us, but now that it was too late to change my mind, a million reasons not to go raced through my brain. The faster we accelerated toward the bottom, the less convincing my reasons for coming felt. The engineer in me studied every rivet, weld, and seal and found them flawless—beautifully designed actually—but that did little to sooth my near-panicked emotional state.

The other fifty people onboard crowded close to the impossibly thin AC glass, gawking and chattering like they were viewing the Grand Canyon for the first time and not an endless darkness illuminated by the blue glow that caught the occasional school of silver herring. The new technology that allowed such a thin barrier had been thoroughly tested over the years but that didn't mean I had to like it. Proven or not, I couldn't help but long for the days when glass for underwater vessels had been four to six inches thick. My father and Jackson stood front and center with the other sheeple, smiling like they hadn't a care in the world, like we didn't just leave Mom, weak and battered by chemo, all alone on the surface.

Her unnaturally thin face was all I saw behind her smile, the smooth skin of her scalp visible through the woven texture of her large-brimmed hat.

"I need you to go," she'd said for the fourteenth time, *framed by the sun like an angel with a halo.*

She'd finally convinced me with her crazy, characteristically unselfish wish that I play nice with Dad and the woman he'd cheated on her with.

"Excuse me, Miss Meadows, but you look a bit peaked."

I stared up into the plastic face of Dr. Candice Lawry, Chief Operating Officer and Artificial Intelligence Guru of Bennet Systems. *Wonderful.*

Candice always looked like she swallowed something horrible but was trying to smile through it and not let on. I suspected it had something to do with being as high-ranking as one can get inside Bennet Systems, yet not being a complete insider, aka literal part of the disfunction that was the Bennet family.

"Thanks," I said, taking the Hydropod she held out to me in the hopes it would be enough to send her on her way.

"Your profile shows you are at an increased risk for DSI," she said, sitting on the edge of the seat beside me and crossing her long legs.

"Depth Sensitivity Illness is a made-up term to excuse the psychological effects of being crushed beneath a million tons of ocean water," I said, taking a sip from the malleable pod she'd handed me. A genius invention, the bubble-shaped object held the perfect amount of electrolyte enhanced water and when it was finished the thin skin remaining could be swallowed as well.

She smirked. "I'll let that comment go, considering the symptoms include lowered inhibitions and heightened anger."

I took another swig, not wanting to feed into it. She leaned in, elbows perched on knees, glassy green eyes unnervingly close as she tapped her thumb and finger together like she had an invisible castanet.

"Let's not have any issues that might spoil this demo trip for anyone. If you feel like you can't control yourself, there's always the option of stasis until it's time to leave."

Did she just threaten to put me to sleep for a month in a box if I didn't behave?

She rose while I remained speechless and cleared her throat to get the attention of the fourteen other families. Bennet Systems, or BS as I lovingly referred to them, was all about family. Frankly, to me, it was more like a cult that kept everyone close enough to monitor. As Candice warned, those who misbehaved were dealt with.

"Welcome!" she chirped in a fake voice that sounded like an animatronic gone wild. "And congratulations on reaching this milestone. You will be the first people to enjoy the new luxury resort, Paradise Atlantis."

She paused for applause.

"We at Bennet Systems are thrilled to be able to offer our very own employees and their families this opportunity before opening our doors to the public. You've worked hard to make this happen, and we extend all the luxury of the finest to each of you in thanks. You will experience AI like never before, as all of your needs are met, and hopefully exceeded, by our artificial staff members. If there's anything you need, just press one of the silver call buttons located throughout the grounds and buildings and you will be showered with assistance. Enjoy the ride, we should be docking in less than an hour."

Everyone erupted into more applause and chatter as Candice waited, clearly not finished.

"One last surprise. We are not the only ones spending a month on Paradise Atlantis."

A hush fell over the shuttle as people began to pay attention.

"The Bennets have decided to join us. Mrs. Bennet wants you to know that you are all part of her extended family."

With this information, Miss C.O.O. disappeared into the crowd, which seemed to swallow her whole.

The entire Bennet clan? For a month? Trapped down beneath the waves with us? My mind immediately went to the only Bennet I'd ever been interested in meeting, Mason. My mouth dried up despite my Hydropod. I'd never been able to string two words together around him. One look at his sparkling eyes or glorious physique and I was destined to become a tongue-tied adolescent all over again.

Pull it together, Sam. I told myself, tightening my ponytail. I needed to focus for shit's sake. I was twenty-six years old and had a master's in engineering in Artificial Intelligence from MIT. I'd be starting work on my doctorate once Mom was healthy again. Not only did I not have time for a man, Adonis-like or not, but I did not have time for frivolities while Mom suffered.

I would simply tour the gallery as often as possible, inspect what I could about the engineering while avoiding certain people, and stay in my room the rest of the time. I closed my eyes and leaned my head back, seeing no reason to keep them open and stare at the dark beyond. Planning would keep me focused on the right things.

"At least somebody here isn't ogling a window with a view of nothing," said a deep voice to my right.

My eyes popped open and took in the face of the dark, handsome stranger. His deep brown eyes reminded me of the woods above land. Thick hair framed his face and carefully trimmed beard.

"Travis Gould." He held out a large hand to shake.

It was warm, but calloused, and he didn't hold back on the strength of the welcome.

"Samantha Meadows," I said. "What department are you in?"

He scoffed. "None. I refused the work study. My parents unfortunately did not. My dad is head of Interior Design, and my mom is the main vital-systems engineer."

I nodded. Bennet Systems notoriously hired females for lead science roles. With the exclusion of my father of course, since he and my mother met Mrs. Bennet back in college. He'd been a fixture since the start, which meant the rest of us were as well.

"Why'd you refuse the work study?" I asked, curiosity getting the better of me.

"I will never work for those assholes."

I smiled despite myself. Maybe we had something in common.

"I don't work for them either," I said. "Dragged here with family, same as you."

The shuttle lurched like it'd been hit by a torpedo, and I froze, clutching the armrests of the seat. My head pounded as my blood pressure skyrocketed.

"You okay?" Travis asked, his thick eyebrows furrowing into one as he stared at my white knuckles.

"What was that?" I breathed.

He grinned and pointed toward a giggling group of girls by the glass. They waved and made silly faces at a dolphin that hovered on the other side. The creature appeared to be smiling ear to ear. I was confused for another moment until one girl put her hand on the glass and the dolphin headbutted it, making the whole vessel seesaw.

"What if it breaks the AC glass? Or it knocks us off course?" I asked, staring at the horrible sight. The engineer in me knew it was a ridiculous fear, but the terrified woman in me disagreed.

Travis laughed, bringing my attention back to him. The rest of my blood rushed to my face and down between my legs when he set his hand on mine. I guess not getting laid in over a year had unfortunate effects on my body.

"It's a dolphin, not an enemy submarine. I'm pretty sure even the assholes could've predicted that. In all seriousness though, are you sure you're okay? If you're afraid of the ocean this is not going to be a pleasant trip."

"Thanks, Captain Obvious. I'm good." I stood up on shaky legs and strode as confidently as possible over to join my father and Jackson. Alyssa was off chatting with Candice, so it was as good a time as any to make a half-assed effort.

"Sammie." Dad held out a hand for me and I took it, forcing a smile. I promised I'd try after all. "Enjoying the view?"

"Jackson sure is," I said, noting my brother's wandering eyes that were locked onto his newest target, a young woman with the body of a super model, too much of which showed beneath her tangerine romper.

My six-foot-two brother bumped me with his hip, making me stagger.

"Are you eight or twenty-eight?" I asked, downing the remainder of my water and popping the rest in my mouth.

My father's smile was worth it though, the way his eyes crinkled when it was genuine always warmed my heart. If only he'd reserved it for our family and not shared it, first with BS and then Alyssa.

"Stand over here, Little Dragon," Dad said, repositioning me with a clear view of the glass. My heartrate sped up, but he held me tightly from behind, grasping my arms for security.

"Dad I'm not twelve anymore," I said, making light of his pet name given because of the way my nostrils flared when I was super angry, like I was about to spit fire.

"You'll always be my baby. Now if you look a bit down and to the left you'll be able to get a first glimpse. It should come into view any minute and this is the prime spot. That's why I've been staking it out."

I bit my lip so as not to make a snarky comment. I promised Mom I'd try. I should at least do so for the first day I supposed.

Within the next thirty seconds or so, a glowing light appeared in the dark waters. As we swooped toward it, the shining bubble seemed to rise from the depths of the Atlantic, revealing a ten-mile-wide snow-globe of something out of a 50's futuristic B movie. Emerald green pastures dotted with bright red and yellow blooms punctuated the circular space. In the center of the maze-like perimeter stood a speckled white statue of some sort. Around it, gleaming silver buildings of rounded glass and metal shone beneath what appeared to be... sunlight.

"How?" I asked, unable to take my eyes off the scene. The cheesy brochure I threw in the recycling can upon receipt didn't do it justice.

"They're called nanosuns," Dad said, reading my thoughts. "I developed them myself. They even dim and wane into a moonlight effect at night that follows the actual cycle of the moon."

It was amazing. But I was not admitting that to him. If that's what started his years of absence from our home—from Mom, then I refused to compliment it.

"Please prepare for docking," Candice chirped.

"Prepare?" I said, unable to control the high-pitched way it came out. "Is it dangerous?"

Jackson laughed, no doubt enjoying torturing his sister. It was like we'd gone back in time to elementary school. I shouldn't have been surprised. We hadn't spoken much since he took the job at BS in our father's department working under him. Better that than in AI with Alyssa. Truthfully speaking, she was closer in age to him than our father. Youngest woman to ever earn a PhD in Artificial Intelligence from Bennet University, she was the logical choice to take over the position from Candice when she was promoted to the equivalent of second in command four years earlier. That's when the affair started and when Mom's first bout of cancer was diagnosed, which made it that much worse. Before that, we'd all gotten quite good at pretending it was normal for Dad to never be around—always working.

I wondered where Alyssa was. It was entirely possible she was avoiding me. That thought brought a big smile to my face.

"You have nothing to worry about, Little Dragon. Just a formality to announce the docking procedure."

I nodded and leaned back into Dad's chest, allowing myself to feel safe for once. It was almost perfect until I heard Alyssa's voice.

"Oh, I'm so glad you two are getting along!"

I pulled away from my dad and hugged myself, stepping far enough away to make a point without saying it. She didn't seem to notice though as she cozied up to him, taking my place in his arms. Her perfect face with her perfect, smooth, dark skin and perfect long lashes, and perfect straight smile lit up as though from within as he rocked her slowly side to side, wrapping his arms around her.

My stomach swam as if the Angelfish outside the closest window had crawled inside it.

"Have you enjoyed the ride, Samantha?" she asked, continuing to beam like a bunch of nanosuns.

"Not really," I said. Dad's crinkle smile faded behind her, and I almost regretted speaking the truth.

Before anyone could say anything else, the shuttle lurched slightly. I tried to convince myself it was another dolphin to slow my heartrate.

But I soon realized that was the ship slowing for the docking procedure Candice mentioned.

It looked like we were about to smash straight into the giant glass bubble when we came to a full stop and dropped downward like an elevator until the view was replaced by a bright green door that slid open to admit us. Smooth as silk, the shuttle slipped inside and the door closed. The water around us drained through the grated floor and a second door opened, offering an upward slope festooned with marble mermaid and merman statues lining the glowing path.

"Impressed yet, sis?" Jackson asked as the oohing and ahhing crowd around us pushed their way outside.

"Too gaudy for me," I said, feet stuck to the ground.

Jackson narrowed his hazel eyes at me and drew a hand back through his tawny hair as understanding lit his face.

"Come on. I'll help you."

Heat rushed to my pale cheeks. I'd never been able to hide a blush, so instead of arguing I accepted his offered hand. It was better than being stuck in the shuttle for a month. I scanned ahead and caught sight of Travis at the top of the incline. His sharp gaze bored into me, causing a tingle of anticipation to spread throughout my body. And together with my somewhat estranged brother, I moved forward, focused on possibilities I hadn't originally considered as opposed to the oppressive view.

Don't stop now. Keep reading with your copy of Lizzy's sci-fi romance LOVE AT 20,000 LEAGUES.

And find more from Lizzy Gayle at
www.lizzygayle.com

Discover Lizzy Gayle's sci-fi romance LOVE AT 20,000 LEAGUES and find more at www.lizzygayle.com

Paradise Atlantis: The underwater, high tech vacation destination where utopia awaits.

Not for Sam. Not only is she deathly afraid of being submerged under millions of tons of ocean water, she's stuck for an entire month with the people she blames for her family falling apart. Even with the unexpected attention of two sexy men, including her longtime celebrity infatuation, Sam is sure the trip will be a nightmare.

She's both right and wrong. A type of pressure sickness she was unprepared for hits Sam hard, causing both lowered inhibitions and blackouts. When she gives in to her desires, a passionate romance blossoms.

Unfortunately, even this steamy new relationship can't salvage the trip when a saboteur uses the AI to commit murder – murder timed perfectly with Sam's mysterious blackouts. Now Sam must clear her conscience by finding the truth. But is she prepared for what she'll find? Because either she's a killer or she's setting herself up to be next on the growing list of victims.

Escape Your World. Get Lost in Ours! City Owl Press at www. cityowlpress.com.

ACKNOWLEDGMENTS

Books are made by more than just an author. A huge thank you to my editor, Tee, and the entire team and family of City Owl Press. Thank you to my assistant, Tiffany and to my cheerleaders: Sarah, Leslie, Kathryn, and Shona. Thank you to Ian and Deborah for starting me off with the Djinn, and thank you to my family for all your support.

An acknowledgements section would be incomplete without mentioning the readers who help me breathe life into the characters in this and all my books. You will always have my gratitude.

ABOUT THE AUTHOR

LIZZY GAYLE loves paranormal so much, she lives it. She is both an author and a psychic. Between mothering her three kids, attempting to understand her rocket scientist husband, and consistently attempting to declutter her home (that she is convinced is a secret portal to a clutter-creating dimension), she does her  best to use her creative gifts and share them with you. Lizzy is a people person so if you contact her, it will make her very happy and she will likely answer while possibly including pictures of her bunnies and/or bird. She has also been known to write Young Adult under the name Lisa Gail Green.

www.lizzygayle.com

facebook.com/authorlizzygayle

instagram.com/authorlizzygayle

ABOUT THE PUBLISHER

City Owl Press is a cutting edge indie publishing company, bringing the world of romance and speculative fiction to discerning readers.

Escape Your World. Get Lost in Ours!

www.cityowlpress.com

facebook.com/YourCityOwlPress

twitter.com/cityowlpress

instagram.com/cityowlbooks

pinterest.com/cityowlpress

Made in the USA
Middletown, DE
22 April 2022

64647531R00132